DEBBY KRUSZEWSKI

Soul Meets Body

Six Degrees of You

Soul Meets Body

©2020, Debby Kruszewski

ISBN: 978-1-09832-971-6

ISBN eBook: 978-1-09832-972-3

Kitten… Follow your heart…
I believe in you. I believe in us.

CHAPTER ONE

~

Maria ran out of the house and sat on the front porch, hugging her knees with her hands and hiding her head on her thighs as she shed silent tears. Her long, lanky legs were the best shield she had from the dust picking up around her. She had wrapped her hair in a cloth to keep the tiny particles from getting buried in it and used the long piece of cloth dangling from it to wipe the tears coming down her face. She desperately wanted to hide from the sights and sounds around her. As the sun was low on the horizon, she unwrapped the cloth and tried to see how long she could stare into the orange ball dropping far off in the distance before it hurt. She wanted just enough hurt to distract herself from her current pain.

"I need to get out of here," she said to herself, shutting out the yelling that came from inside the house. She felt the difference in the air as it went down further and further while the dust continued to whirl around her.

The side of her face still burned from when her father struck her with a hot pan days ago. Her tooth was cracked and likely would remain so since they couldn't afford to get fixed. She continued to do her best to clean it and hoped it wouldn't get infected. She had endured all the pains from the beatings so she could shield her sister and mother from getting hit.

But today, she just couldn't do it. The loud bangs and screams coming from inside made her jump. There were not many places to hide there, and he knew them all. She felt in her heart that there was a better life for herself, and she would find it one day. Her younger sister Doris cried out her name for help. She just couldn't do it. Not today.

The sun now looked just like an orange slice. It felt so close she could almost taste it. Her mouth was dry from crying and lack of water. The pounding in her head didn't stop.

Her father was also tall as she was. He was handsome with his narrow mustache and thinly trimmed beard. He turned into a monster at night when the sun was setting, and he was home from a long day in town. No one really knew or understood what he did; they were not allowed to ask many questions.

He dressed in silky button-down shirts and trousers. He flirted with all the ladies in town while Maria's mother labored in a factory and pretended not to notice. It makes you wonder if Maria and Doris were a mistake. Was their mother disappointed because she had thought having kids with this man was her answer, her ticket out of poverty and working long hours in hazardous conditions? When she first met him, little did she know she was going to work harder than expected, and he would beat her and her children a few times a week. She was tired and aged way past her 35th year. She was defeated years ago when Maria was old enough to take some of the pain for them, and she would rest in her bed and cry as she listened to the screams. She would drift off into her dream of her husband being entirely different than the monster he had become.

Maria became tough and took the pain as a badge of honor for the family. She wanted to be strong and help her mom, shield her sister, Doris. Maybe one day she'd see her mother smile and play with her and Doris as she did when things were good. Maybe one day her mom would be happy. As Maria got older, the badge fell off her uniform and she also became weak. She understood the defeat her mom had experienced. It wasn't easy and today was not Maria's day for another beating. It was someone else's turn.

An eerie silence came from the house behind her. She figured that there was no more energy for them to cry, and he had probably become too tired to hurt anyone else. The door slammed as he left the house. This time, he did not return. It was safe now, and they could breathe again.

It was just before Christmas, and on the island, they didn't have Christmas trees like they did in America. Only the rich families could afford to have them imported. Her father didn't spend his money on them. Maria's mom made do with palm trees and ornaments. When Maria came back into the house, their tree was on the floor, its ornaments crushed and sharp. It was an obstacle course to walk through without getting cut. Christmas was not going to be celebrated this year.

"When I go to America, I'm going to have a big Christmas tree with ornaments and presents under it," Maria said out loud days after the last beating when the bruises were starting to turn a greenish/yellow. Their pain was slowly fading away.

"Shut your mouth, Maria; you're not going to America. You'll stay here and work like everyone else. Stop your dreaming!" Maria's mom shouted at her and left the kitchen.

Maria's sister turned to her and held her hands. They sat under the light bulb hanging over the table on a thin wire. "I believe you'll make it to America; I know you can," Doris said with hope in her heart.

Maria took her upstairs and tucked her into bed. "Tell me more about your dream, Maria," Doris said. Maria smiled at her as she leaned in to shut off the light on her nightstand. She sat on the edge of the bed and tugged the sheets around her sister to keep her in tight.

"Another time, Doris." She turned off the light and went into her room. Each night Maria prayed she could one day go to America. She had dreams but no longer wanted to share them with her family since her mother kept shooting them down and making her feel guilty for having them. There was a young boy she dreamt about and felt in her heart. She knew it was her son.

"I'm coming for you, baby. I'm going to give you the life that you deserve. I promise."

That summer she worked at the local grocery store bagging groceries and then was moved to stocking shelves. When she turned sixteen, she was allowed to work the register. She also babysat the local neighbor's kids. Each peso she made she put into a box hidden under her bed. Maria did any job she could to make money to get herself to America.

I'm coming for you, baby; I'm going to take care of you. I'm going to America.

She recited it to herself over and over. She kept her dream of having a boy inside her heart, but she never gave up on herself. She never gave up on God's promise.

Maria watched the neighborhood kids and tucked them in bed too some nights. Their mother handed her the pesos she was owed one late evening, and Maria ran home. Their house was calmer now that her father had left them. Maria and Doris now lived alone with their mother who did her best to work hard and provide for them. Maria opened the door just as her mother turned on the light and sat at the table with the box in which Maria kept the pesos she had earned.

"Why are you hiding money from me?" her mother demanded. Maria stood in shock, sickened that her plan was ruined.

"Momma, I been saving up…"

"For what? America? You really think you're going to go to America? What about us, what about your family? You're not going to America."

Her mother was stern and held onto the box. Maria stood in silence as she stared at it, thinking about how she could grab it from her and run away, but she didn't. Maria sat down at the table and tried to reason with her mother.

"Momma, I want to go to America. I just feel that is where I need to be. You're not going to stop me."

Her mother glared at Maria, took the box tightly in her hands, and rose up. "We need this money for a new roof. You're not going anywhere," she yelled as she stomped upstairs, furious with her daughter.

Maria remained at the table and cried. There had been enough pesos in that box to begin planning her trip to America.

I'm not giving up; I'm not giving up on you, baby. This is just a set-back. I will get there, baby, I will.

She took the money she made that night and put it in a book. She knew that now she needed to find a new place to hide her hard-earned money so her mother could not find it. The game plan had to change. *I will get there; I will, s*he chanted to herself in her bedroom to help her fall asleep. The next day she went into town in search of new jobs to get herself there.

CHAPTER TWO

~

In her junior year now, Maria sat in the schoolyard with a group of friends who all believed in her dream. They did their best to make it to class daily but were frequently called to a job to help their family and could not make it. They struggled. They sat around a tree and discussed their what-if-I-lived-in-America dreams and made a pact to see the journey happen. When Maria told them about how her mother stole her money and that now she needed a new job to make money to replace the lost pesos, they put their minds together on what she could do.

One of their better ideas had to do with the laundromat at the far edge of town. The plan was for her to bargain with the owners to go and collect clothes from some of their customers and wash them herself. She found a few families and single men who worked in the fields who had no time to wash their own clothes. Maria left the house early in the mornings to collect the bags of laundry the people had set out for her. She carried the heavy bags herself to the Laundromat and washed them before it was even daylight. While they twirled in the machines, she worked on her homework from the previous day. When the clothes were done, Maria ironed and folded them, delivering them before her first class at eight-thirty. Maria planned out which families she could cover every day and still be able to make it to class. The pay was not as good as she hoped, but when the word got out about how reliable she was, the clientele expanded. She had an overload of work.

Some days after school, she still worked at the grocery store until closing, and on her way home, delivered groceries to mothers who had several children and ran errands for some of the wealthier families. One family paid her to cook a few meals for the week for them, and she became quite good at it. The pesos continued to come in. Maria gave some to her mother to cover expenses; then she hid the rest. When she was about to turn eighteen, she had enough money to make it to America—almost nine hundred US dollars.

"I can do it. I can get there," Maria confided in her friend.

"Where will you go? Where will you stay?" her friend asked.

"I don't know. Miami? New York?"

"I have a cousin in New York. He lives on the upper west side with a bunch of people that are just like you. They wanted to make something of their life in America." She wrote his name and phone number on a piece of paper for Maria. "Call him in the evening late, he works three jobs and usually gets home after midnight."

"I can't call him that late! It is so expensive. What if I miss him? Will he even know who I am?"

"Then write him first. Set-up a time to talk. He understands. He went to America by himself to follow the same dream."

"Thank you, thank you. I will!" Maria ran home with Jose's phone number and address in New York. *Wow, New York!* she thought. The dream was coming together.

She started writing the letter:

Dear Jose,

I'm a friend of your cousin, Diana. I want to come to America and have saved up about nine hundred US dollars. I'm turning eighteen years old next month and am willing to work hard. I have several jobs here that I do—I clean, babysit, cook, and work at the grocery store. I'll do what I need to earn my keep. Can I come and stay with you until I get myself on my feet? I promise I won't stay long. Please help me. I must leave this place. I will stop at nothing to get there. Can we set up a call? I'll call you and pay the fees. Thank you, Jose. Whatever your answer is, I thank you.

> With love and respect,
> Maria

She addressed the envelope carefully and left the house early in the morning to do her daily laundry and make it to the post office before class started. She didn't care if she was going to be late. This was the first chance she had to get to America. At the post office, she paid the postage and kissed the letter off, finally feeling at ease.

"Baby, see I'm working to get there, baby boy. I am going to America and make all my dreams come true. I'm doing this for us, baby," Maria said out loud on her way to class that day. She continued her routine for the next few weeks, checking her mailbox several times a day. No letter came back. The mornings became hard. The long walks dragging the laundry from her client's houses to the laundromat became difficult and were starting to take their toll on her. One day Maria tripped, dragging a large bag of laundry just before the sun came up. She busted her lip and knee and felt defeated. She laid on the dirt road and started to cry.

"Jesus, please help me through this. Please, I am trying so hard, please help me through this."

She sat for a few more moments and got herself together. Maria used her shirt to wipe the blood that was dripping from her lip and planned to wash up at the laundromat. As she started down the block, a man yelled out behind her, "Maria! Maria!"

She turned around to see who it was. It was her father. She quickly fixed the bag and strapped it to her back and turned around to continue the walk to the laundromat.

"Please go away, please go away," she yelled as she walked as fast as she could, hoping to lose him.

"Maria, Maria!" he continued to call out as he raced to catch up with her. "Let me help you." He took the sack from her, and she was defeated enough to let him help. He had been leaving the bar that he partly owned when he had spotted her. Today he was surprisingly not as drunk as she had expected him to be.

"I've been watching you, Maria. You're very determined."

"Thanks," she replied but would not look at him. She had to get the laundry running, do her homework, deliver the clothes to her customers, and make it back to school.

"Let me help you with your wounds." She pushed him away as she moved into the bathroom at the Laundromat and quickly closed the door behind her. She cried as silently as she could from the pain of cleaning off her cut up knees and thinking about the fact that he was trying to help her. When she came out, he was gone. She was hurt and relieved at the same time. She had no time to dwell on it and quickly began putting the clothes in the washer. When the clothes came out of the dryer, she hurriedly ironed them. She gathered the clothes together in a sack, locked up the laundromat, and turned around to leave. Surprised to see a bike at the front door with a bow on it and a basket in the front, she wasn't sure what it was about or where it came from. Her father stood in front of his bar down the road and leaned himself on the corner of the door.

"Go and take it, you could use some help," he yelled out to her. She was stunned because she really needed the bike. She looked at it and then back at him. "I really need this bike. I really need to do this to get my dreams. How can I take this from him?" she said to herself, confused as to what to do.

"Why are you being nice to me?" Maria screamed across to him. He dared to take a few steps closer.

"I haven't been the best father to you and Doris. I haven't been the best husband to your mother, and I stole her dreams. I don't want to steal your dreams. I know you want to get to America. I want you to follow your dreams. I want to say I'm sorry." He held out his hand toward her and then was afraid she wouldn't accept it, he folded his arms and looked down.

She nodded to him as she put the sack in the basket, got on the bike and pedaled away to drop the laundry at the clients' houses, and then raced off to school. The breeze in her hair felt good in the hot, still air. She felt guilty but also relieved. She needed his support.

It is just a temporary solution to get me to America; I'm coming, Jose; I'm coming, baby boy. I will make it happen, she told herself as she entered her class that morning.

CHAPTER THREE

~

The next week she followed her usual routine, and on her way home from school before heading to the grocery store, she made a quick check of the mailbox. The letter she was waiting for finally had arrived. "Thank you, Jesus!" she screamed and tore open the letter. It was from Jose.

Dear Maria,

It is so nice to hear from you. I am so happy to hear that you are interested in following your dreams to come to America. It was very difficult when I first arrived here, and I understand how you will need some help to get yourself started. I have a few roommates, but if you are not afraid to sleep on the floor and fight for the bathroom in the morning, you are welcome to come and stay with us. I can do my best to get you a job waiting tables at the restaurant I work at. I also can help you get into a secretary school sponsored by our church and will help you get a day job. You'll be on your own in no time. I have a monthly call to Diana's family on Tuesday the 30th at midnight, your time. Go there, and we can make arrangements. You will be very happy here in America. This is where dreams are made!

With much love,
Jose

Maria read it repeatedly to herself and smiled. "I'm going to America; I'm going to America!" she chanted to herself. The 30th would be in two weeks. She felt impatient but knew it would be there soon enough. She ran to the grocery store where Diana also worked. They stocked shelves in between the time they spent working the register. On their break, they hurried to the far back aisle and sat behind the meat freezers, and Maria showed Diana the letter. "I'm going; I'm going!" Maria said as quietly as she could.

"Girls, there's someone at the register!" The shout came from the front of the store. The girls hugged each other and giggled as they scattered to the front. Maria smiled and began waiting for the call. It could not get here fast enough.

It was Tuesday the 30th and Maria was up half an hour earlier than usual at four am. She just could not sleep out of pure excitement. She had been able to double up on the workload after she received the bike. Now she was so grateful and excited to have it. She rode off, determined to get the laundry done quickly. She didn't notice her father watching her as she swept by him on her bike. He smiled as he was proud of her consistency and knew she was up to something. The late afternoon turned into evening as the quiet stress from her anxiety began increasing. The clock could not move fast enough for her. After the store closed, Maria and Diana went to Diana's house to await the phone call. They sat at the phone and stared it down.

A few minutes after midnight, the phone rang and Jose was on the other end, sounding like he was oceans away. Her parents spoke to him first, keeping the call short since the charges added up quickly. Diana said a quick hello and passed the phone to Maria. She waited for this moment for two weeks and could hardly believe it was happening.

"Hello!"

"Hola, Maria! So, you want to come to America? Okay, well we are ready for you. When do you plan on coming?"

"I turn eighteen next weekend; then I graduate high school in a few weeks. I will come afterward."

"Good, let's stay in touch. I don't have a phone, but you have my address. I will call again next month, and you should have a date by then. You will have to get a visa. I can have my church sponsor you. I know the church you belong too. I will have it arranged, but you are going to need your birth certificate to bring to them. Can you do that within the month?" Maria was hesitant as she didn't own a copy nor knew how to get one. But she knew of one way.

"Si" Maria said reluctantly at first, but then replied again with confidence. "Si!"

"Okay then, ciao!" Jose hung up the phone, and Maria stood there amazed at what had just happened. She had just made a pact to go to America!

CHAPTER FOUR

~

Maria decided to train Doris on her laundry route as her sister would need to make money for the family when Maria headed off to America. It was hard for the fifteen-year-old to get up at four-thirty in the morning and work all her jobs and still go to school, but she did it. Doris was quiet and a bit shorter than Maria, but she did want to learn the routine. It just took her a bit longer than her older sister. Maria hoped that she could grow the thick skin she needed to do the job, because it had to be done. It was coming time for Maria to leave, whether the family wanted her to or not, but Maria didn't want to burn any bridges. It wasn't her style. She wanted to keep her reputation in her homeland even though she knew it would work out in America. It had to.

Maria's father walked out early each morning as Maria made her way to the laundromat. She mostly just nodded at him, and he nodded back. When Doris was with her, he would wave and say hello to her. She didn't know how to react. Maria talked to Doris in the laundromat and let her know it was okay to forgive him as she had done.

"What would Momma say?" Doris asked upset and dedicated to their mother. She had every right to be.

"She has to make her own peace with him. Let him apologize; and once you accept, if you accept, I think it will make you feel better. Help you move on with your life. Don't you have dreams, Doris?" Maria asked gently.

"No" she responded. "No, I will stay here and take care of Momma." Her reply was not said in disappointment but in what is expected of her. She shrugged and looked down. Maria gave her a kiss on her head and hugged her tight. She didn't want to upset her younger sister.

While the laundry was running in several machines, Maria looked out to see if she could see her father from the doorway. He stepped out often for his cigarette time. She ran over to him in hopes that she still had his support and could get a copy of her birth certificate. She stood behind him, waiting for him to turn around.

"Hello, Maria," he said before he even turned to smile at her. He lit his cigarette and waited for her to speak.

"Hello. I need your help. You can't tell Momma. I need a copy of my birth certificate to get my visa. The church is going to sponsor me. I haven't told her because she won't let me go. Can you help me and keep it secret?" She was nervous about his response but confident that she was going no matter what.

"Of course, Maria. I told you I support you in your dreams. I will help you. Can you help me? Help me to ask for an apology from your mother? I want to turn things around. I really do. What do you say?" She felt the side of her face and remembered the last time he hit her. He watched her warily. She decided she had to let go to move on.

"Yes, I will help you," Maria said with confidence.

By that time Doris had all the clothes folded and stacked up on the bike. She walked it over and greeted their father. He put out his hand and she accepted it. And so the forgiveness began.

Days later he walked out of the bar on an early morning and handed Maria an envelope with her birth certificate and some cash.

"Thank you. I leave in the middle of the night on the 15th. I'll leave Momma a note and sneak out. Fix the roof for her. Don't ask any questions, just do it." Maria said to him, and he smiled.

That was something he could do. In the next few days, he showed up at the house with a crew when she was at work and started working on the roof. Maria's mom came home from work with groceries she had picked up from Maria at the grocery store. Tired and ready to make dinner, she looked up and saw him there fixing the roof. He waved and she didn't know how to react. But she smiled.

After a few days, she brought out lemonade she made fresh. After a few more days he joined her for dinner as the sun set. This was the distraction Maria needed.

CHAPTER FIVE

~

The date was set, Maria was eighteen now and could do what she wanted. There was a future for her in America, she knew it. Jose was going to meet her, get her a job, and she would stay with him until she was on her feet. The time drew near, and she packed a bag quietly in the middle of the night. She said goodbye to the things she would miss—her favorite doll, the dogs, her childhood. She said her last prayer in her bedroom, thanking God for this opportunity. Maria took one last look around and left an envelope with money for Doris by her bed. She went down the stairs to leave for good. The light in the kitchen went on as she entered the room. It was still dark as night out. Her mother appeared at the kitchen table. Maria stood frozen.

"So, this is it. You're going to America?" Caught. She didn't need this roadblock. The point to leave in the middle of the night was to avoid the confrontation with her mother trying to hold her back. She had a love for her family in her heart, but she had a dream and promised her future baby that he would grow up in America.

"Yes, Momma, I'm going to America. I didn't tell you because I knew you would be angry with me. I want to prove to you that I can make it. Doesn't Frank Sinatra have a song that says, 'If you can make it here you can make it anywhere?' or something like that? I'm going to New York and will be staying with Diana's cousin Jose. He's getting me a job and into a trade school through the church. I'm going to make it, Momma,

I promise. I'll send you money and bring you there if you want too. I will. I need to do this for my child and me. I'm going to have a son. I know it; I feel it in my heart. I want this for him. I can't live here; I will die."

Maria's mother took a deep swallow that was so loud Maria could feel it. The sweat beaded up on her forehead. She was so nervous about what her mother would do next.

"Alright then. Do you have enough money?"

"Yes, I've been saving up and working hard. Doris is going to take over my jobs here, so I don't burn any bridges. She's good; she can do it. This is where she wants to be, with you. She can do it, Momma. And I will make it. I know it." She stood stiffly waiting for her mother's reply. This was the most confident conversation she ever had with her mother.

"Good, good. You have been working hard. Make sure you take care of yourself and go to Mass on Sunday. Don't give up on God. Make sure you call us often and keep us in your heart."

"I will, Momma; I will."

"Good. So, Maria, I will miss you for sure. I have something for you." She went into a drawer in the kitchen, took out an envelope hidden behind the silverware, and gave it to Maria. "Take it," she said as she looked Maria in the eyes and did her best not to show any emotion. When Maria opened it, she was in shock. It held the pesos her mother had taken from her a few years back. It was the gift Maria did not expect.

"Thank you, Momma, but please. I want you to keep it. Use it for yourself. The roof is fixed now. I will be okay. I know I will be okay." Maria handed her back the envelope and gave her a kiss and a hug. It was time to go.

Diana had borrowed her Dad's truck to take her to the airport and off they went. It was the longest ride across the island they had ever taken. When they arrived, both of them were nervous. They hugged as Maria grabbed her bag from the back and knew there was no turning back. When Diana pulled away, Maria started her chant again.

"Baby, we're doing it. It's time. I'll find you. Thank you for believing in me!"

She excitedly boarded the plane and never looked back.

CHAPTER SIX

~

After arriving in New York, Maria met up with Jose at the restaurant where he worked at night. He was on his lunch break from his construction job but wanted Maria to meet the owner and get started working right away. He was very kind to her. She was set up as a waitress and enrolled in school to get herself an office job down the line.

At night she slept on the floor in the living room with another couple as the three men shared the bedroom together. Another woman came to stay with them on the weekends, but then she left when she found a boyfriend on the other side of town and stayed with him. They were all in the same boat. They went to America to follow a dream.

Maria woke up early in the mornings as her body clock had been set at four am for so long. She used that time in the bathroom before the others got up and then did some studying. She cooked breakfast for everyone. On a nice day, Maria went for a walk before class and enjoyed the new experience of having downtime. Even though the streets were dirty, and the smell from the excessive traffic was pungent, she knew there were better times around the corner. She just had to keep believing.

One weekend Jose decided to borrow a truck from a friend. They all drove to what they called the suburbs. It was quiet, the houses were big, and they had beautiful views of the water.

"This is what I want, Maria. I want to live out here and raise my family," Jose said. They walked on a beach where rollercoasters were roaring in the background. "I'm saving up and working towards partnering with the owner of the construction company where I work," he continued. "I'm going to be able to run his next big project. It will be a big promotion, so my salary will be significantly better. I'm going to land myself here. What do you think?"

Maria wasn't sure if he were asking her for permission or if she wanted to be a part of this dream. "It sounds lovely Jose, good for you." She left it open-ended.

The weeks continued, and the weather started to get cold. The apartment was getting tight. The couple whom Maria shared the living room with wanted to get married but could not afford to leave the apartment just yet. It was becoming uncomfortable for Maria to be sharing the space with them, so she picked up extra shifts at the restaurant to avoid being there. The money was okay; it helped her save up quickly.

One evening the restaurant hosted a party that took them into the late night. She worked it alone with the bartender, Dario, whom she did not know all that well. He was tall and had a nice smile. Maria was focused on her studies and making money. She wanted to get out of that apartment soon to get started on her life.

"Maria, don't forget the limes on that," Dario said to her as he called her back to the bar to top off the drinks. She was eager to serve the drinks and get back to the apartment to sleep. They were both exhausted.

"Oh, thank you. I'm so tired," Maria said as she came back holding her tray steady. He smiled at her and hoped that she would notice, but she didn't. The night dragged on a few more hours. When the party table was good and drunk, they left a nice tip. Maria and Dario started to clean up and count the money.

"Maria, sit and have a drink, put your feet up. I'll clean the tables." She was stunned by his statement and so exhausted she took him up on his offer. He smiled again, and this time she caught it. Maria poured herself an iced tea, took off her shoes as she sat at the booth and counted the money.

It was double what they would have usually made on a Tuesday night. She leaned back and dozed off without even knowing it. It felt good to get some rest in the quiet. Dario cleaned the area and smiled as he looked over at her. When he had finished and was ready to close up, he came over to touch Maria's leg. She was so peacefully resting.

"Maria, Maria," he said softly as not to startle her. She was startled anyway and embarrassed as she did not realize she had fallen asleep. He smiled at her again; she smiled back giggling.

"I'm sorry, but I'm sure you want to get home to rest," Dario said.

"I'm resting here. Can I just stay here tonight? I'm so tired and so sick of sleeping on the floor." As she knew it was not an option, she giggled and got herself up. "We made a lot of money tonight, so it was worth it. Thank you for cleaning up, Dario."

"My pleasure... So, Maria, since you don't want to go home, can I interest you in breakfast? I mean it is morning? My treat." She was stunned by the invitation and didn't know how to handle it.

"Yes," she said and then was shocked that she agreed. Dario was charming, very charming, and seemed to have a bit of class to him that the others didn't. His shirt was nicer than the others. He wore a gold chain. His teeth were all real. She had found most men to have false teeth from not taking care of themselves because they couldn't afford to do so. Dario's hair was groomed back. He was for sure different than the other guys she had met there.

They went to a local diner, and as tired as Maria was, she was also starving. She was thin from all the work that she was doing and not eating properly. When the food came, she ate like she had never seen food before. He noticed and laughed.

"You must be very hungry, Maria. Make sure you chew first." She stopped herself out of embarrassment and did as he said.

"Please forgive me," she said after she swallowed the mouthful she was working on.

"Don't worry, I'm only making a joke and was afraid you might choke." He smiled again; she smiled back. They shared small talk and their stories. He was from a wealthy family in Venezuela and came to America to go to college. He was in his second year at NYU in Manhattan and working to pay off his tuition since he didn't want any money from his family. He also wanted his independence from them. She was impressed and felt that she wasn't good enough for him. She wanted more, and he made her happy. She didn't know what that emotion was, but she liked it.

He insisted on walking her home and pulled her close to him, so she could rest her head on his shoulder. She gladly obliged. She felt safe with him; it was warming and comfortable. They both didn't want the night to end.

"So, Maria, you're going to go and sleep on the floor in Jose's apartment next to a couple. That can't be comfortable." She sighed as he spoke because she was dreading it at the same time.

"Yeah, I guess so. But I have saved up a good amount of money and hope to find a better place soon. I saw an apartment with two other women available. I should be able to get the money together by the end of the month."

"Then where will you sleep? On the floor again? In a room with someone else? What kind of dream is that?"

"Well, well. You're right, it's not like my dream. I guess I dreamed of coming here, and I didn't get much further than that. You're right. I'll look for something that's a bit more comfortable."

"Maria, you work so hard. You have worked so hard for so long. You are a smart, beautiful woman. I don't want to be so forward, but I do like you. I do have dreams of working in the stock market when I graduate. I work on an internship now a few days a week. I have big plans. I'd like to see you again; maybe you can start your dreams with me in them?" He leaned in for a kiss, which felt so warm and so right.

"I can start dreaming with you in it." He smiled back at her.

"Now, Maria, come home with me. Not for anything else but to sleep. You can have my bed, and I will sleep on the couch. I promise I won't try anything. Don't you want to get some real sleep and not wake up so early to fight for the bathroom? I live alone; it will be peaceful, I promise." The offer was tempting. She was so tired and sleeping on that living room floor was depressing. She hesitated as all she could see was her mom disappointed at this moment and yelling at her for not going to church as she had promised. But it was tempting. He was kind; she really liked him.

"Yes," she said. She became a woman of little words when she was with him. They went to his apartment, and as promised, he kissed her again goodnight, gave her the bedroom and her privacy, and he slept on the couch.

Maria crawled into Dario's bed. His sheets were soft and just the right cool temperature to let her body relax and fall asleep. Maria laid on her back with the sheets slightly over her face. The pillow was fluffy and had a faint scent of Dario. Those few moments she slept and didn't dream of anything but happiness.

Dario awoke her deep sleep in the morning and sat on the corner of the bed as she came to the realization of what a good night's rest felt like.

"Good morning," he said and handed her a coffee.

"Good morning," she replied with a smile. Again, she was embarrassed to be enjoying herself.

"Looks like you slept well."

"I did, thank you so much, this was a wonderful gift." She started to get up and get herself together to rush out to school.

"Wait, wait, it is still so early. I know you don't have a class right this minute. You have some time. Stay with me. Let me make you something to eat. Please, I enjoy your company and beauty. It would delight me for you to stay." He dashed his smile again which he had learned she could not resist. She stayed for a breakfast that turned into dinner that evening, the next evening, and the evening after that. Eventually, the nights in his apartment became nights in his bed with both of them occupying the space.

"You are my special charm, Maria," Dario told her one night after dinner.

"I think you are mine. I never met someone like you before. You make me smile so much. I'm enjoying this. And you are right: I need to continue building my dream. I don't know past coming here, but I do want more. I want to get married and start a family. I do. I can feel that. I just don't know what that means yet." She looked down as she was embarrassed to put all her cards on the table to Dario.

"I want to finish school, get my dream job, get married, and start a family," he said. "I want to have it all with you, Maria. Do you believe in me? Because I for sure want to have you as part of my dream."

They became serious pretty fast. She thought it must have been meant to be. That night Maria went to Jose's apartment and packed her bag. She left a note for Jose with the rent for the rest of the month, a thank you, and a goodbye.

CHAPTER SEVEN

~

Dario graduated with honors from NYU and got a job at a bank. Maria worked in an office and spent a few nights taking classes there. Dario pushed her to want more for herself, and so she was using her hard-working determination to get herself there. They both worked the weekend nights at the restaurant for extra cash. Things were starting to pay off. After a year, Dario worked himself into a promotion, got on one knee, and asked Maria to spend the rest of their lives together. She answered with a happy yes.

The ceremony was quiet, Maria's sister came, some of Dario's family came along with a few friends. They held the reception at the restaurant they worked at and went on a honeymoon to a quiet bed and breakfast in Connecticut.

One night after dinner they stood on the deck of their room that looked out onto the ocean. The sun was setting, and she stood in front of him as he looked into her eyes.

"We have a big future ahead of us, Maria; I'm so lucky to be spending it with you."

"I could not imagine it any other way. You made my dreams come true," she replied softly.

The music played in the background. They danced together as she closed her eyes and said to herself, "I *am here for you, baby boy; it is all coming together. I'm waiting for you."* They continued to dance until the cool air became too much, and he carried her inside.

In 1970 after Maria graduated with a BA from NYU, Dario received another promotion, and they gave birth to a baby boy named Maximo. He was long and lengthy, much like Maria. His dark hair was full and his dark eyes made her smile. They moved into a bigger apartment with the dream to one day live on the water in the suburbs they knew as Westchester.

This was where my story began.

CHAPTER EIGHT

~

I was born on a rainy day in the spring just after Easter. I felt the love from my mother before I even knew her. Her voice was sweet in my ear. She smiled each time she said my name, touched my face, sang me to sleep. As much as she meant to me, I meant more to her.

Today I am lying in bed with my wife draped beside me. My long legs scrunched into hers as they sometimes felt too long to be in this bed. I'm caressing her arm as she sleeps soundly. When I stopped, she started to fidget. When I gave her a soft kiss on her hairline and continued the strokes, she calmed down. Blake has been in my dreams ever since I was a little boy. I dreamed of this woman in my arms, her blonde hair smelling like a tropical forest. She was always my dream. I'm forever blessed.

Rain was beating on the window ever so lightly as it is again early spring. It was my birthday two days ago, the same day my mother passed away. I lay here awake, dreaming of her and how I lost the first woman I ever loved. I can't sleep thinking of how we'll bury her today, and I will have to give a speech to send her off. I didn't know how to do it. I stopped caressing Blake's arm again as I was so indecisive over this. Blake took notice and this time was bothered enough to open her eyes. She didn't have to say much because she understood what I was going through. She has always been my rock. Blake moved to give me a kiss and held my face close to hers.

Afterward I finally closed my eyes and started to relax by following her breathing techniques she practiced with me to calm me down. We didn't even need words anymore. We were in sync. I gently pushed her over, so I was leaning against her, and we shared the last moments of the morning in a light sleep. She held me just tight enough and took her turn at caressing my arm. We have always been good at switching gears. It gives me the comfort I need.

CHAPTER NINE

~

My mind went off into my younger world when we were a family with my parents Maria and Dario, even my brother Nico. I was so happy then. My mother was my best friend. She stayed home with me in my early years. We would go to the park; she took me to museums as she wanted to learn more about the culture. We sang on the subway. At night, after dinner, she tucked me in and read to me until I fell asleep. In the mornings she was always there for me when I awoke. I felt so safe and warm. She was everything to me.

I was king of the castle in our house. My dad dropped his bag when he came home from work to grab me for a hug and sit on the floor and play with me. When I was older, we hit baseballs. My parents bought me a bike to ride. It was perfect for when we spent so much time in the park. Although living in the city, I had the best backyard. After a couple of years, I had a companion—my brother Nicolas "Nico." I was not sure of him at first. So much attention went to him, but I was still Mom's favorite. We still read at night, even if he was in her arms. Dad played catch with me when he came home from work. When Nicolas became old enough, we played together. He was finally ready to be a playmate. Things were alright. Life was good.

My parents were very much in love when I was young. I remember that. The way my dad smiled at my mom each time she walked into a room was magical. She knew how to press his buttons and how to make him happy. She made his favorite dishes when they fought and snuck into the shower on early mornings when they thought we were sleeping. It was special. They went on date nights that excited us because Nico and I then had the chance to have a babysitter who let us stay up late and play video games. When we heard them turn the locks on the door, we ran into our beds. We giggled as they came to kiss us goodnight, knowing very well we were not asleep. They smelled of smoke and booze. It was like they had this amazing adventure. Sometimes they went out dancing, sometimes just had dinner. Mom was funny after a few drinks. She laughed so hard and held onto my dad so tight. After our goodnights, they shared another drink and slow danced in the living room. We watched from the door until we got caught. They laughed away. Sometimes we joined them and laughed with them. Their cigarette smoke filled the room, and we also felt drunk and fancy as we all danced. Those are the memories I miss the most.

My dad got another promotion up from the trading floor, past a desk, and into an office. He was so proud of himself. Maria was too. She made his favorite dishes, but the job demanded him to stay late nights at the office and sometimes to entertain clients. We had dinner alone many nights, but over time it was noticeable that Dad was just not around much anymore. He didn't ask her to accompany him to client dinners; when she did go, she felt out of place. He made sure she noticed that. I could tell that she was hurting. At night, Dad sometimes came home for just enough time to shower and head back out the door. She cried herself to sleep. I crawled into bed with her and cried too. I cradled myself into her until she finally fell asleep. When my dad came home and saw us, he smiled and thanked me for taking care of her. The dream was fading. I didn't know how to fix it.

My mom picked herself up and decided to get a job to learn what it meant to be out there and what she lacked to gain her husband's love back. She wanted him to look at her the way he used to. They became just roommates. I watched her and supported everything she did. She got her hair done a certain way, changing the color, used new lipstick, and wore higher heels and outfits that to me seemed way too flashy. My mom was becoming someone I was starting not to recognize. When my dad came home, she would attack him; it was uncomfortable. He was rough with her but not abusive. He treated sex with her like he was angry. At least that's how it felt listening through the wall. She came out of the room like she had been hit by a truck. Sometimes she came into the kitchen and just sat at the table with her lipstick smeared and her hair a mess. The cigarette was lingering in the air with the ash falling onto the table. I sat with her and held her hand. I didn't know how to fix it.

After a few years, right before I was to decide where I would go to high school, my father came home and asked my mom for forgiveness for not being home and becoming the family man he promised he would be. This forgiveness came with the promise of keys to a house in Armonk. It would be big enough for my brother and me to have our own rooms. There was a backyard for us to play in, and the public high school had a football team. I didn't know what we would do with all that space. I was comfortable with our apartment. I loved sharing a room with Nico. We talked at night and played catch in the dark. We read to each other and talked about girls. I felt like the new house was a lot of space to distance all of us from each other. We already were spaced out living in this small apartment. What would happen? I was afraid that this blessing would be more of a breaking point.

My mom was excited, as she saw this as a means for everything to go back to normal so they could continue the dream they had together. Then it began happening again. My dad worked late, and I could tell that he stayed out with work events to prevent him from coming home. I stayed on the couch one night to wait for him. It was as if I were the parent, and he was a kid missing his curfew. His shirt was open, and his tie was messed up. He walked in and smirked at me; I did not break into anger, but it showed on my face. He sat down across from me on the couch.

"Are you excited to move? Armonk, you're going to love it there…" He went on and on until I stopped him.

"Why are we moving to Armonk? Why can't we stay here? I like it here. All my friends are here. Why don't you come home at night? Why are you breaking up our family?" I was demanding answers. He sat with his hands across his legs and bowed his head down. He knew I was right.

"I'm sorry, son, just doing my best to provide for all of you. I want you to go to that prestigious high school and have a nice life. You can go to the really nice public school in Armonk if you want. I want to give that to you."

"Don't blame this on me. I have the opportunity to go to a private school right here in the city on a scholarship! I don't want to go to your obnoxious public high school. You're ruining our family." I got up and went into my room, slamming the door. Everyone was already awake. I didn't care. If he wasn't going to be good to my mom or us, I wanted him to know it. I was so angry.

Weeks went on, and my dad came home more often. He retreated to drinks in the living room with an undesirable number of cigarettes that lingered on all our clothing. It was almost easier for him to be working late. My mom, of course, did everything that she could to make him happy—his favorite dinners, the massages afterward, and the seduction that was again, cringeworthy as it was so desperate. Then she had exciting news to share just a few days before we were about to move into our house in Armonk. We sat in a land of boxes, not exactly knowing what was what. Eating cereal with a fork, it was a tension we were all ignoring.

"Everyone gather around, I have something very exciting to tell you!" We dragged ourselves into the kitchen. I wanted so badly for this to be some good news. We really needed some good news.

"What is it, Maria?" my dad asked her. We all eagerly awaited her response.

"Well, I am excited to announce that we will be having a baby right after Christmas!" There was a silence as Nico and I were in shock at the thought that this house and baby were going to make it all better. It wasn't going to work, but my mom really believed that it would. I pretended for her that I was excited, and Nico followed my lead.

We went to bed and played catch in the dark. We listened to our parents argue, but they were trying to keep it quiet. We didn't feel good about any of this. It was so hard to watch my mom become so hurt and lost from my dad. I didn't know how to protect her. It was upsetting.

The moving van pulled up to a four-bedroom house in Armonk. We walked in as if we were in someone else's house. My dad was so proud of himself and smiled as the boxes were unloaded from the truck. I didn't like this house and felt like I didn't belong there. I wanted to go back to the city and play football with my friends. I didn't want to be there. My brother and I took a walk around the block to check out the neighborhood. It was quiet. It creeped me out.

I started at the local high school. I felt tall and gawky, but somehow I discovered girls—blonde girls, brunette girls, red-headed girls. They all wanted my attention. I didn't understand it, but I liked it. I made friends with a few guys, tried out for the JV football team as a freshman and made it. I was becoming someone, and I started to like it. Life was not so bad in Westchester. My dad came home most of the week at a decent time. My mom was starting to show. I thought maybe I was wrong; maybe this white picket fence has something to it. I walked girls home after practice when they stayed to watch. I had girls doing my homework for me, even though I was smarter. I didn't care—I wanted the attention. It made me feel the way I did when I was a kid and my mom and dad danced until dawn and stared into each other's eyes. I wanted that.

I danced at homecoming with the most beautiful girl I could find. She had flowing blonde hair and a dazzling smile. She had breasts when the other girls didn't, and she let me touch them whenever I wanted. She taught me to do things I could only see on HBO. I dreamt of this. Then came the invitation to her house for dinner, and as I still was learning what to wear to fit in, I did my best to be polite. Her parents smiled when they opened the door. Then their faces went from excitement to frowns. Dinner was just as uncomfortable with awkward conversation as they passed along the potatoes. I didn't know what I did wrong. Then after a few days, she broke up with me because "Daddy didn't approve."

"Maximo, I mean I like you a lot. But, hmmm well, you aren't really that smart, and you look at other girls, and I just don't."

"Don't what? I'm in advanced classes. Some girls help me with my homework because they like me and I let them. I hold my own in class. Is that what you're upset about? Really? You knew that when you met me. I don't get it."

"Well, you are just not someone I can see fitting with. I mean I like you. But my dad will kill me if I see you again. You're just not like us. I hope that we can still be friends."

I stood up and walked home, leaving her in the bleachers in the field. What? So, I am not good enough? I don't get it. I was like a king last week, what is this? I was so upset it just made me want to go and sleep with another girl and keep flipping through girls in this fashion. The story always became the same. I'm just not Irish, or Italian, or rich enough. It was never enough. Never. I was crushed. I went home and slammed the door. It felt like no one was there. I sat at the kitchen table, and after some time I called for my mom. Usually, she was at my beck and call when I come home. Today I didn't hear much. Nico came to the top of the stairs.

"Maximo, come up here. Mom is bleeding and moaning. It's something with the baby." I frantically ran up the stairs. I could not bear something bad happening to my mom. I just couldn't. When I appeared, she called for me, and I ran to her and hugged her as tightly as I could.

"Call your father! Please! Please!" Nico ran to the phone to call and left another message with his secretary. She was unamused by our cries and needing him right away. He was nowhere to be found. I ran to the neighbors who called 911. She was raced to the hospital where she had a miscarriage. Our chance at salvation seemed to be slipping. My mom stayed in the hospital overnight. Dad never came to visit. We left messages at his office one after another; finally, his secretary let us know he no longer worked there. I didn't know what to do. I held it from Mom. She came home, and I took care of her as a private nurse. She was so grateful.

Days went on, and my dad did not appear. I asked my neighbor what to do; I could not keep this from my mom much longer. As we spoke, his car pulled up into our driveway and I ran to greet him. I was so angry and glad to see him at the same time. It was overwhelming. He grabbed me from the back of my neck and brought me in for a kiss. It was awkward. He was weird. I could tell he had been drinking, smoking, and no idea of what else. But it was a lot. I didn't want him to see Momma, not like this, but he went straight up the stairs to her.

"Dad, did you get my messages? Did you?" He didn't answer. He just went to her. She awoke and turned to him as he came towards her. She started to sob as he held his head on her stomach and begged for forgiveness. It was bigger than losing the baby.

"Maria, I love you. I love you so much. I am so sorry. I am so sorry; I have failed you." She was in pain and wanted him to leave her alone to rest and politely tried to push him off. It was hard to notice that she wasn't pregnant anymore. Watching him, I knew that he had never gotten the messages. He didn't know about the miscarriage. Even in pain she still cared for nothing but his feelings. Nico and I stood at the doorframe and watched this show; it was painful.

"Maria, I have to tell you. I'm a horrible person. I lost you in my heart. I was unfaithful, now I must pay the price. I have been having an affair with my secretary and lost my job because of it. She is also having my baby. I will get another job, and I will take care of this baby as well. But I am going to live with her. I will always love you, Maria, and our boys. I will do the best I can to take care of your baby." As he spoke, I was ready to come at him and punch him in the face. He did not know about the miscarriage. She never gave him the messages.

"Oh, *my* baby? *My* baby? Not *our* baby? Get out, get out of my house you bastard." He got up and looked at us. Nico cried and ran to her as dad stood in amazement. He came to me for comfort and some sort of acceptance to this apology. He would not get it from me. I walked down to the front door and held it open for him. As he came to and walked into the open space, he held his hand out to me.

"You don't even know?" I said to him as I was raging and trying to not cry like a slobbering mess in front of him.

"Know what, Maximo?" He would have to learn on his own, more than anything that I think he is a bastard. I punched him in the stomach that pushed him out to the front of the house, and I slammed the door in his face.

CHAPTER TEN

~

As the school year moved on, Armonk was growing old, and my popularity was diminishing. Christmas came and went, and Mom fell deeper and deeper into a depression. I went straight home after school to be able to care for her. She laid in bed most days; I watched movies with her and made dinner. This depression was deeper than I could handle.

"Mom, can we go back to the city? I hate it here. You're so unhappy; I hate school. Nico isn't doing well. Let's just go. Maybe it will make you feel better." She didn't respond but turned over and went back to sleep.

I went to sit on the lounge chair across from the bed she laid in. I started an art class that I was not that excited about. Our assignment for the week was to work on a sketch of something vulnerable. I couldn't put my finger on what that was until this moment. I took up my sketchbook that for the most part was blank and sketched my mom—her body limped over onto the side of her bed, hiding her face from the world under the pillows. She faded fast.

I spent the night working on my drawing and when I felt it was finished, it was past our dinner hour, past our bedtime, and past the anger I had for the situation. Nico came in from time to time to check in on us. He was lost. Mom slept and didn't move much. She didn't eat much, but she was still alive. I'm grateful that she was still alive.

My sketch had depth in the lines, darkness in the body, and the emotion portrayed perfectly. I was proud of this piece. There was a part of me that wanted to get to school to show it off. I needed my confidence back. I was falling into my mom's depression with her and needed to be pulled out of it. I let my mom sleep through the rest of the day; and in the morning, I forced her to get out of bed and shower. Eating was at a minimum, but she was now at least eating something. Nico cried a lot about it. When I needed a break, he came in to sleep with her. He may be better at cuddling than I am. Morning was approaching, and I would start the cycle of taking care of her. I need a better plan to get her out of this funk.

When I arrived at my art class right before lunch, my anticipation was strong, and I was not paying attention to most of the people surrounding me. I hoped that my novelty of being the new guy had worn off; I was sick of being used. I really didn't want to become close to anyone. I was ready to get back to my life in the city, back where I belong.

"Nice work," she said to me as she leaned over my shoulder. It was the princess I dated when I first got there. She was for sure pretty. Her blonde locks had mesmerized me. I was so hurt by her. She wasn't the girl in my heart any longer. She used me and I didn't know it. I realized that being with her made me feel all the hurt I held inside right now. My dad had hurt all of us — me, my mom, and Nico. It hurt to watch my mom and my brother hurt. I needed to be strong for them and stay on top of this. I needed to get this situation into a better place.

"Thanks," I replied without paying her mind. She still hung on my shoulder, and after a few moments I was able to smell her hair and feel her breast pressed into my shoulder. I gave her a push away.

"What's wrong, Maximo? I thought you couldn't resist me." She was fishing. "Why don't you ask your dad if you can be allowed to flirt with me?" She moved herself to make sure I could see her breasts popping out of her shirt. I was unamused. She responded with a smirk and a wink as she turned swiftly and headed toward her seat across the room.

Class began. We all showed off our work and the story behind it. Right at the end, it was my turn.

"This is an important piece of vulnerability to me because it is my mom. She suffered a miscarriage when we first moved here. At the same time, my dad left us to be with his new girlfriend and their baby-to-be. My mom has stayed in bed ever since. So, I captured the moment and hoped that I can use the hurt and pain that I feel for her to put it onto paper and have it escape me." I stared into the clock as I didn't want to make contact with anyone.

The class stood in awe of what I had presented. I came in as the new kid, the great personality that lit up the room. (Well, that is what Blake always says I do.) I was the star athlete on the field, the guy all the girls wanted to know. I was the charmer. I never felt so at peace and relieved after I gave that piece to the class. I don't know how easy it was after that. Only since that moment, I am only vulnerable with Blake.

"Wow, wow. Maximo. This is unbelievable. I didn't even think you were into this class. You really have captured a moment. I'm proud of you. Can you stay for a few minutes after class? It's all good." I nodded that I would. The bell rang after a few more students spoke, and then they all ran out. I stayed in my seat, the first seat towards the front at the window. The room once upon a time was a science lab and it was still set up that way. I sat patiently at the stool and waited for the class to empty, and she came over to me and took a seat.

"How are you doing, Maximo? It can be therapeutic to get out your anger and frustration on paper. This is amazing; it really is. But I can feel your pain. How are you doing through all of this?" I looked down as I wanted to cry and scream, I felt so mad. So, I looked down and kept it together. I could not let my guard down.

"I am alright," I said, looking up as high as I could. I was not able to make eye contact with her.

"I don't believe you," she replied. I chuckled and held my face in my hands as I was starting to cry. I talked myself out of it. *"Stop crying, stop crying, get it together."* I finally got it together and was able to show my face.

"I'm good, thank you. I'm good. I didn't know that I would enjoy sketching. I want to continue."

"I think you should. If you want to talk, Maximo, I'm happy to listen. Maybe you should get some help?" I stood up and faced the window. I didn't want help from anyone. I picked up my bag and started to walk out of the room. "I'm good, thanks!" I waved and walked as fast as I could to lunch. I just wanted to avoid the topic. *Make it go away, make it go away. God help me get us out of this. Please help me.* I was praying quietly now for months. *I do not like to live out here. I want to go back to the city.*

I watched the clock in each class. I just wanted to get back to my mom. *Did she go back to bed when I left her? Did she even dry her hair? I hope she won't catch a draft and get a cold. Will she eat something? Should I make her soup?* I want to sketch. I want that alone time to dwell in my pencil and pen. I want to continue to look into how we can get out of this. *I'm going to take care of you, Momma; I promise I will."* The bell rang, and I jumped a bit. After I ran to my locker to grab my sketchpad, I headed straight home. I needed to get Nico from school and get back to Mom. I worried as the day went on that she would be alone too long. I raced my fast walking bulldozing on my plan. Then there she was. Princess. Ugh, she was persistent.

"Where are you going so fast, Maximo?" She stood leaning on a tree waiting to seduce me. I ignored her and kept on my way.

"Maxie? Where are you going? Don't you want to play with me?" She started to chase after me. I continued to ignore her.

"Maxie, I can drive you. Why don't you let me take you? We can pick up your brother." She dangled her keys to her fancy car in my face as she walked backward in front of me.

"NO, I am not interested. And DON'T call me Maxie!" I politely stopped her and moved her out of my way. I just kept walking. She stood in the street amazed that I had told her no. Others stopped to watch since she never was refused. It was a moment she didn't believe would happen to her. She was irresistible—her hair and the breasts. She was what most guys my age wanted. It was hard to say no. But in my head, it wasn't her.

The picture of the girl I wanted, the woman I wanted to see her develop into was not her. At this moment I can feel that she is not my future. The woman I have in my head was starting to make herself present. I needed to know how to get to her. I felt myself looking into her eyes, but she was still a blur. I needed to find her; she was so close to me right now.

"Maximo, I'm waiting for you. She is not what you want, I am. I want to be with you, Maximo. Follow my voice. I will wait for you." I heard her. She made me smile. I stopped in my tracks to close my eyes and feel her. I felt her. Who is she? Who are you, my mystery woman?

"I am listening, my love, I know she isn't you. I can hear you. I can feel you. What do you look like my love? Oh, don't tell me. I want to be surprised. I will know. I am waiting for you too."

I stood on the sidewalk basking in this conversation in my head. My eyes closed and my breathing began coming back to a normal rhythm. She knew how to calm me, and I didn't even know her yet. I can't wait to meet her.

The car horn beeped loud. Then there was the princess in her car, chasing me to my brother's school.

"Hey, Maximo, sorry. No more Maxie, I promise. Let me take you to pick up your brother. I can even let you drive." She didn't give up. I don't even have a license!

"No," I shouted at her and started to walk faster, cutting through backyards to avoid her. She slammed her hands on the steering wheel and gunned the motor. She wasn't good at losing. She never had it happen before. I grabbed Nico at school, and we raced back home to check on Mom. We were so afraid that the more time we left her alone that she might do something to harm herself. Last week I had hidden all the knives in the house. I felt silly doing it, but I did. As soon as we entered the house, we could smell onions and garlic in the air, coming from the kitchen. I could hear my mother singing. Nico and I look at each other in surprise, dropped our book bags, and ran to her.

"Hello, boys! How was your day? How are you doing? I decided to make some of your father's favorite pork chops. He's coming for dinner. Please go and get washed up and started on your homework." She flashed a smile and just like that she had broken out of her spell of sleeping beauty. Nico took it all for face value and ran up the stairs. It was the white picket fence he wanted back. I didn't want it.

"What? What is going on? You're all dressed up and cooking? You've been dead for the past few months. He calls and says he's coming over, and you are magically okay with this?"

"Yes, I am, Maximo. He wants to make amends. We all make mistakes. We have a nice house here and a nice life. Let's not be hasty as to what this all means. Just be happy and forgive your father. That's what God would want you to do and what I want you to do, okay?" she said as she was stirring the sauce she just made. Her lipstick was perfectly lining her lips. She slowly sipped on some wine. I could tell she was nervous and really wanted to believe all the words she had just said. I was mad all over again.

I stomped up to my room and took my sketch pad and pencils out. I decided to draw her—the girl in my head...the one I wanted...the one I feel I'm destined to be with. *"What do you look like love? Can you come to me? Help calm me down and take me away from this moment. Follow my voice, my love. I need you to take me away from this. I'm ready for you."*

With that said, my hands started to sketch as if I were just sitting there watching myself draw. But it started to come together. I went into the details of her eyes, the flecks within, the pupils' depth, what they look like when she looks at me. Her wavy hair was long, past her shoulders. I didn't get to the nose and the mouth. I couldn't see it yet. But I could see her eyes. I closed mine to picture her further. I felt as if I were in a dream state. I started breathing at a slower pace. I saw myself running through a field that led to the woods. I could see an image of someone in front of me. I was chasing after her. She was beautiful, and I didn't even know her. I don't know what she looks like. I can smell a fruity smell and taste the more I think of her. She turns around and gestures me to keep chasing, and I do. I can't run fast into the woods. But I don't stop.

"Find me, Maximo; I'm waiting for you."

It made me smile. All I could think about was her. The forest was deep; it was starting to get dark, but I was not afraid. I was not leaving. I was calm and collected. I didn't want to leave this vision, although I didn't know I was in a vision. I got close enough to hear her breathing as she ran. Her hair bounced as she moved, and her flowing white dress moved up as she ran. I was close enough to touch her; then I was awakened by my door opening so loudly it almost made a bang.

I gasped for air like I was in the water, submerged by a crash of sorts, coming up for air and not knowing where I was. I was in so deep, and she was so close. My sketch was outlined—her hair and her eyes in depth, and her nose and mouth sketched out. I didn't even know what I drew. I had the definition of her dress: the blouse opened with strings hanging, the lines in the fabric like white linen, the ruffles along the collar. She had become so real to me. I didn't look at who was at the door, I just stared at the sketch. She calmed me right down.

"I am coming back for you my love. I will find you," I said with my eyes closed. It was a moment no one could take away from me.

"I didn't know you were an artist, Maximo." It was my dad. I suddenly became startled and wanted to hide the sketch. I was vulnerable to it. She was my secret. I didn't like people to see my work, and I wasn't ready to share her. She was mine. She was my secret.

"God, help me find her. I need to find her."

"Come down; your mother made a fabulous dinner."

"Why are you here? Why are you back here?"

"I wanted to see you. I wanted to see your mother. Is that okay?"

"What about your new life? New family? I thought you forgot about us. We haven't heard from you since you left."

"We can talk about it when we go downstairs, okay?" I didn't like or appreciate his vague response. I knew I was not supposed to hate my dad, but right now I detested him with all my being. My mom was a mess because of him. *He can magically come back, and now she is okay?*

When we sat down for dinner, it was awkward. My mom and dad were giggly teenagers again. Nico was happy again. *How can this just happen?* I was not happy.

"What's going on?" I asked. I didn't believe that this could be real. *He left us, how can she just welcome him back?* Everyone continued to chew on their food while I just pushed it around on my plate.

"Well, Maximo. I understand your concern. I called your mother today to talk to her, and we had a lovely conversation." Both of them looked at each other and smiled.

"So, I did make a big mistake. I understand that. I lost my job because of it. I was living with Briana and our new baby, Safaia. But I realized that I was still in love with your mother, and I wanted to make it work. I spoke to Briana, and she will raise our child. I will be able to see Safaia under an agreement and pay her child support. I have a new job, a better job in Manhattan, and we will rent this house out and go back to living in the city. What do you think?" I looked at my mom who was gushing over my dad's every word. She believed in him; I felt it. She wanted this dream. She wanted her Dario back. She wanted to smile again.

"Mom, how come when I said to move back into the city, you didn't want to?" I screamed at her.

"That's not true dear; I was just not sure what was going to happen. I'm happy to go back to the city. I think I'm going to start working again. It will be good for us to start over. I accept that your father made a mistake, and we'll conquer this together." She grabbed his hand and held onto it. It was as if she needed reassurance to follow the plan. I thought it was stupid. The past few months I had seen how weak my mom was. I wanted to help her and be the salvation for her. I had thought that I was.

After dinner, my parents giggled at the dinner table when Nico and I retreated to our rooms. Eventually, the giggles came up the stairs, and their bedroom door slammed shut. I could hear her loud laughs. Nico came in to sit with me.

"It's good to have them back together. Aren't you happy?" Nico asked. I didn't want to lie to him, but I didn't want him to be sad.

"Yeah, I guess this is great," I told him. But I kept my focus on my sketchpad. Nico threw his baseball to the ceiling. And we listened to the laughter in the other room we weren't supposed to hear.

CHAPTER ELEVEN

～

We moved back to the city. I was slowly breaking down and joining in the happiness. My parents were in a normal family routine. It was hard to believe it was true, but it was happening. My dad started a new job that brought him home at normal hours in the early evening. My mom started to work at a law firm as a paralegal. She enjoyed it. It kept her interesting and gave her stories to tell when she came home. Our family life was coming together. The school year started, and I went to a prestigious private high school. I was still girl hungry but being in an all-boys school with uniforms helped me concentrate on school. I was still very interested in art and signed up for as many art classes as my electives would allow me. We were back in football season. The cheerleaders from a sister school would stand on the sidelines. As the weather became colder, their skimpy uniforms couldn't keep them warm. It became easy to have them snuggle into you as you offered them your jacket. I was hungry for the girl in my head. I did not stop at trying to find her amid the blondes, the brunettes, even the redheads. They all looked at me. I had my pick even when I thought this all-boys school would not offer me such an option. It seemed to be easier here. My family life became quiet, and my dating life began. I was back to being the star again. I was enjoying this season.

There was Rachel. She was a brunette—not really my thing, a little chunkier than other girls. I enjoyed her curves. She was insecure and gave me almost anything I wanted. I frequently dazzled my fingers under her skirt; there were times she seemed uncomfortable and uneasy about it. I asked her if she wanted me to stop. She would cringe and say, "Keep going." But I could see it in her face she wasn't ready for it. I decided it was best just to push her away. I was falling for her though. She was kind and really liked me. But when I stopped calling her and talking to her after the games, she became further insecure and was upset with me. I just didn't want to hurt her. She was too sweet and kind. I was just a young boy who wanted to experiment with girls. I didn't want to hurt her in any way.

Weeks passed by and Rachel finally took the hint and stopped calling. My mom gave me a nasty look each time she said: "No, Maximo is not here. Can I take a message?" She didn't want to see another girl broken.

"Why are you ignoring her?" Mom asked me.

"I just don't want to hurt her. So, I broke up with her." I really didn't, but this was the best way I knew how to not hurt her. I walked away.

The next day I went to school and was killing it—got an A+ on my calculus test and was crushing it on the field. That afternoon I was called to the Principal's office during gym class. I had no idea what it was about. I was a star athlete, got good grades, all AP classes. What could I have done wrong? I came in with a chip on my shoulder as I figured it must be something good. It wasn't. I walked into the Principal's office and was asked to sit down immediately. I did as I was told.

"Maximo, we have a code of conduct here at this school. All boys who go here are privileged and are expected to respect the code. They are asked to sign a contract on this code. Do you remember this?" He handed me the code of conduct that I had signed when I arrived at the school.

"Yes," I replied. I had no idea what I had done. My brain was going crazy, and my hands were getting sweaty. I was so nervous I was rubbing them up and down my thighs. I was sure by then my face was stark white, but I was not sure what I had done.

"Do you know this girl?" He handed me a photo of Rachel. The good girl. . .the one who I didn't want to hurt. . .the one I didn't want to push to do something that she didn't want to do. . .the one I let get away so I would not hurt her.

"Yes, Rachel." I didn't want to give out more information than that. Was she hurt? Did she get into trouble and bring me into it? I was at a loss of what was going on.

"How would you say your relationship was with Rachel?" the principal asked.

"Well, we dated a little bit. Rachel was a very nice girl, but it just didn't work out." I sat back in the chair. I was vague; I don't know why. I am just nervous and confused. I wanted to ask questions, know more. Why was I there? I didn't ask. I was sure I was about to find out.

"So that is it? It didn't work out?"

"Yeah." Should I have said more?

"Well, let me ask you. Did you maybe go out with Rachel because you felt she would be easy? Maybe try to push her to do something she didn't want to do? Maybe try to be cool in front of the guys on the team?"

"What? No, no, not at all. She wanted to do more, and I asked her each time if she was comfortable and she said yes. I really liked her and didn't want to hurt her. Maybe I wasn't ready for more, so we just stopped talking."

"Really, well her story is very different. Let's be honest here. You could have any girl you want, why did you choose her?"

"She was nice, and I think she's pretty. I liked that she liked me."

"Well, she and her parents see it very differently. They are asking to press charges against you, saying that you tried to force her to have sex with you. We do not stand for that here at this school. You are here on a scholarship, but we don't condone your kind here. Lots of these boys come from very nice families in Westchester."

"I just moved to the city FROM Westchester. I stopped when she said yes, and her eyes said no. I walked away. I don't understand why she's accusing me of this. I promise you it's not true. I would not treat a girl like that."

"Well, it is your word against hers. Rachel's family is very prestigious and gave a large donation when her brother graduated from here a few years ago. I'm going to call your parents and let them know. Let's all try to work this out under the radar, so this doesn't get around."

"I didn't do anything! How do you not believe me? Seriously? Because my parents didn't make a fancy donation? I'm a good student and earned my scholarship. I am your star quarterback, but I'm not good enough?"

"Maximo, don't make a scene." I was fuming at this point. I was so enraged. How dare she!

"Maximo, I suggest you do not contact her, and you are suspended from the game Friday night. We will get this underway next week. If anyone asks why you cannot play, you'll tell them you had a death in the family."

"Yes, sir," I managed to say, but I was livid inside. I stared out the window to prevent me from jumping him across the table and screaming in his face. Maybe hit him. But I got myself together and nodded my head and left. I slammed my hand into the lockers as I walked down the hallway and back to my class. I avoided everyone as now I was asked to lie by the fine private institution I attended. I waited for the bell and when the last class was over, I grabbed my bag and ran out of the back door and home. I was so upset I cried, and I was embarrassed that I was so emotional over this. I really liked Rachel. I really did. I really didn't want to hurt her at all. I stopped. I played the last time I was with her over and over in my head. I saw the look on her face and I stopped. Is she doing this because she didn't want me to stop? My reputation will be ruined. I have to figure this out.

I turned to my sketching. I went back to the sketch of the girl in my head—the woman I can see in my future. *What do you look like? I need you right now. Help me, I need you.* I waited and concentrated on the outline of her lips, the definition of her lines that drew close into her inside we never get to see. I want to be able to taste what her lips feel like. I picture them to be soft and warm. *Oh, find me. Find me.* I drifted off as I closed my eyes and fantasized about her. What will I do when I get to meet her face to face? I imagined her and wanted to touch her lips. I wanted to draw them as perfectly as I could see them.

"Maximo! What is this disturbing phone call I received this afternoon from the principal's office?" my mom said as she barged into my room unannounced. I quickly sat up and covered my sketch since I didn't want her to see it. I stood up, hoping I could grab her to calm her down and explain.

"Mom, I can explain, I can. Mom, I didn't do it, I swear. Please listen to me, please." She kept cursing in Spanish. I let it go until she was tired enough to stop.

"Mom, please," I whispered and clenching my jaw to keep from losing it. She stopped the cursing and sat down on the edge of the bed with her hands folded across her chest.

"I'm listening."

"Thank you, thank you. I never hurt Rachel or forced her to do anything she didn't want to. I was hooking up with her, and she would push me to do more. I would ask again as I tried, and she insisted to keep going. Mom, I saw the look in her eyes as I was up her skirt, and I didn't want to push her. I didn't want to be someone that hurt her. She wasn't ready, so I stopped. Mom, I really liked her and respected her enough not to hurt her. So, I stopped and then I blew her off. I thought that was the right thing to do. I don't know why she's saying that I did something to her. Do girls really think this is how to get a guy back? I didn't do anything to her! I don't understand why she's doing this. Now I can't play on Friday." I started to cry and moved over to look out the window. I was embarrassed to have to tell my mom this story. I knew she'd be mad at me.

"I believe you, Maximo," she said. I was astonished. I turned around and stood in front of her.

"Thank you, Mom, thank you." I came in for a hug.

"Sounds like she didn't get what she wanted, and this is how she knows to hurt you. I bet she is a really rich white girl, huh?"

I chuckled a bit. "Yeah, how did you know?"

"I know what you like. I see you look at girls. So, is she the girl that you keep drawing?" She was sneaking to uncover the sketch pad I hid when she came in.

"No, no, no. It's not her. I do like her though. She's not the girl I draw."

"So, who is the girl?" I was hesitated to answer. Do I sound crazy that I am drawing a girl that I have in my head? That she talks to me? That I can taste her when I close my eyes? That she is all I ever wanted? Okay, right. That sounds crazy.

"No one."

"Oh, it seems like she is someone. You get lost in your thoughts when you're drawing her. I see the look in your eye. I had that once. When I wanted to come to live in New York, I saw you. I talked to you. I knew you were coming to me. I knew with you in my heart I would come to America and meet your dad. Then, there you were. I felt connected to you before I knew you. I had you in my heart. You are my angel." I was blown away. I never had heard that story before. She understood me. I felt close to her again because she knew what this was.

"That's exactly what it is. I don't know why, but this girl came into my head. I believe she talks to me. I can't get enough of her. I think about her all the time. I'm working on picturing her as close to what I can. It's not Rachel. It's not any of the girls I ever met. But I want to find her. I see my future with her. Is that crazy?"

"No. It's not crazy. Follow your dream. You'll find her. Don't let this Rachel ruin you. I'll talk to the lawyers at my firm and see what the best way is to approach this. I will not let her ruin your reputation at this school. I love you, Maximo, don't forget that. You were in my heart before I even knew what a dream was. God knows what's best for you. If He put a promise in your heart, He will make sure it happens. Keep your trust in Him." She touched the side of my face and held me close. I was still crying from the fact that I was understanding the bond my mother and I have. It is special. I remember being a little kid and how she smiled at me, and I felt so warm and comfortable. This feels the same. I was so happy that she believed me. I stayed in my room to continue my sketching, do homework, and gather back my confidence until dinner time.

Dad came home as we were eating. He seemed distracted; it was a familiar cycle I don't want to remember. Mom explained to him what happened with Rachel, and Nico listened attentively.

"So, Dario, I spoke to the lawyer I work for. He said they have crossed a line here. He is going to go in with me and Maximo to 'discuss' the situation and let them know we will not be bullied. We want him to play on Friday in the game and not have his reputation tarnished." My dad listened as he ate dinner and poured himself a beer.

"Alright then, it looks like you all have it figured out. Good," he said as he retired to the living room. He was distancing himself again. I watched him from the wall as he drank his beer on his lazy boy chair and talked to himself. He was strategizing. *Was it about work? Was it about us? What could it be?* I wanted to know him, so I stared at him until he noticed me.

"Maximo, I can feel you watching me. Come over." He signaled his hand although he didn't look my way. I went over and sat on the ledge next to him. He looked at me; fear was in my eyes. *Was he mad with me about Rachel? Did he care?*

"So, what is this Rachel thing? Should I be worried? This is a fancy school. I'll talk to your mother. If we need to hush this situation with some money to the school, I'll do that."

"Dad, I didn't do anything, I didn't. I swear. Mom believes me, and—"

"Listen, Maximo. I was a young boy once upon a time. I understand. You're curious; you like girls. I saw the picture of her. She's not so pretty, but I understand she's rich. You're not poor. It's sad when people use money to manipulate a situation. She's learning an ugly trait way too early in life. It'll ruin her if she keeps doing this. Don't lead with money. It ruins people. When they think you don't have any, they treat you a certain way. When they think you have money, they treat you another way. Watch and remember that. We'll go to the school tomorrow and settle this. I don't care what this lawyer has to say. I'll take care of this. You're my son and I'll take care of this. You'll play on Friday, and Rachel will be put in her place."

"Dad, I didn't do anything. Don't you believe me?"

"Don't worry about what I think. Just know I'm bailing you out of a situation. That's all you need to keep in your mind." He dismissed me, and I headed for my room. I was not sure if I hated it more there or back in Armonk. My dad did not believe me, and it hurt. He told me not to lead with money and then manipulated me with money. He should practice what he preaches.

The next day my parents went to the principal's office. I was not invited. I sat in class anxious as to what the conversation would be like and how each player would handled it. Did my mom stand by my dad, or did she lead with what the lawyer told her to do? Did he write a check? What will be my punishment, the price tag for this? Social Studies right now was just not going to be retained in my brain. Before the bell rang, I was called to the principal's office. My parents sat there looking very pleased with themselves.

"Please, Maximo, have a seat. So, your parents and I had a great discussion about you. I can see how this may be a misunderstanding. I'll need you to apologize to Rachel. After that, you're welcome to go back to the team and play in Friday's game. Besides, the team needs you." Everyone smiled. I didn't know what happened; I hadn't done anything wrong. But I went to Rachel and apologized. She tried to hook-up with me again. As she came in for a kiss, I pushed her away.

CHAPTER TWELVE

~

There were other girls after Rachel. We won our division championship in football; before I knew it, Junior year was at an end. My friend Jax asked me to work with him at a beach club in Westchester.

"I hate Westchester," I told him. We had played together on the football team; he seemed to be the only friend I was close to. He was real and not a jerk like the rest of the guys. I played politics with them. With Jax, I didn't have to.

"Come on. No, you don't. Besides, it will be fun. I did it last summer, made some nice extra cash. Had fun with the crew, come on. You'll like it—a new place to party, meet girls. What do you say?"

"So, what will we be doing?"

"Grunt work, putting out beach chairs, doing gofer kinda stuff. I like to work in the kitchen and hope to get a job with the chef. You can work the tables, things like that. If you can lifeguard or caddy, they're hiring for that too."

"Yeah? I actually can do both. Alright, let's do it." We went down to fill out some paperwork on Saturday. It was that simple. I had my driver's license by that summer, so my mom let me use her car. It was too good to be true.

The first few days were cold and rainy as it was just turning from spring into summer. The job sucked; the people sucked more. Demanding.

I worked all over the club during the day, and at night I waited tables. The cash was good; the girls were hot. Older girls, younger girls, mothers. They were all good looking. I got a great tan and was having a blast with this crew. Pool parties, after everyone left, went on almost every night. I was getting drunk with a girl on each arm. I didn't even know their names. I didn't care. I was enjoying the time. Somehow it helped me avoid what was happening at home. I had a different perspective on Westchester. I was the man. I lit up the parties, experimented with drugs, and learned to love to smoke cigarettes and pot. I wish that summer never ended.

Back at home, things slowly went downhill, but I was ignoring it. I was hardly ever there and came in at all hours. My dad yelled at me in the mornings as I dragged my ass out of bed. Sometimes I didn't come home at all. I would stay with whatever girl grabbed my attention. My dad wasn't home much either.

Nico was lost. He went to a summer school program and drowned himself in school. It didn't come as easy to him as it did for me. He was upset with me because I was not around much. He made sure I knew it. I had a Tuesday off and took him to the beach. Just us. We threw a ball around and jumped waves. We stayed to watch the sun set as we sat back in beach chairs with some music playing. Sometimes I didn't know who we were more like or dad or our mom. Nico was a loner, and it felt like my fault. Maybe he was more like Mom.

"So, Nico, are you mad at me?"

"I don't know. I just want to be older. I don't fit in. It's lonely. The house is so quiet without you. Dad goes to see Briana and their child. Mom is working late nights so I eat dinner alone. I'm jealous that you are working and having fun. I guess I have to wait to grow up."

I put my hand on his head and messed up his hair. I hadn't seen how quiet the house had become. I banked on Mom always being around; I just wanted to avoid Dad.

"I'm sorry, I'll try to be home more often."

He smiled at me. We went back to the city and to an empty house. I made dinner for us, and we watched a movie together. Nico was sad. Mom didn't come home until late and was surprised to see us both at home. She was frazzled when she came in. She had been drinking, and I could smell the cigarette she smokes when she goes out.

"Hi, my favorite boys, how are you? Both together, well, this is a treat." She stumbled a bit. Her lipstick was no longer on. I noticed that her shirt was misbuttoned.

"Mom, what's up? You alright?"

"Oh, of course I am, my dearest." She stumbled over to kiss me. She was off. I followed her to the bedroom and helped her get undressed and into bed. As she got into the sheets, she was falling in and out of conscious. Nico came to watch at the door. I sat by her and rubbed her arm.

"I love you, Momma, are you okay?"

"Yes, baby. Thank you." Then she was fast asleep. Nico looked down in disappointment. Later I helped him get into bed. I laid next to Nico in his bed, as I was feeling the loneliness this house brought.

"Does Mom come home like this a lot?" I asked Nico, really not wanting to know the answer.

"Yes." We stared at the ceiling and fell asleep.

The summer was crazy and loads of fun because I avoided what was going on in the house. As time went on, we got used to Dad not coming home again. No one asked questions anymore. Nico started to slack off and leave the house. He didn't want to be home either. When the fall came, I was back at school and a normal life schedule. Football was where I hid; I had new girlfriends that occupied my time. I also drove to Westchester on weekends to hang with that crew.

I decided to take my date to the house where we used to live in Armonk because I wanted to show off a bit. Since my dad still owned it, I felt I had the right to drive by and let her know it was mine. I was curious about what new cars were in the driveway and the family that lived there now.

When we drove by I saw Briana in the window, but she didn't see me. He told us he rented it to a nice family. Did he mean his other family? Did he live there? I was so upset to see her and my dad's car in the driveway. He had lied to us again. I was so upset, I couldn't let my date see me get red and steaming. I told her I didn't feel well and quickly drove her home and went back to the city fuming.

I came into the apartment and slammed the door. Nico was home alone. I didn't want to upset him as he was struggling with schoolwork. I took my anger the best I could to a place where I hoped he would not see. I sat with him as he finished his homework. Then my dad came home. We hadn't seen him in days. Now I knew why.

"So where is your mother?" he asked us.

"I don't know, I guess at work?" Nico said as if he were afraid to answer. Dad laughed as he took his hand to wipe his face. He paced back and forth.

"Yeah, work, uh," he said and laughed to himself some more.

"So, Dad, why do you suddenly care? You're never here. Don't you have another family? Maybe another family back in Armonk? What is it about that place anyway?" I demanded. My dad stopped in his tracks and came right into my face. He tried to hit me and stopped himself in his tracks. I was acting brave, but I wasn't. I wanted to take it back.

"You know that I have Safaia, you know that. I don't need you to remind me. But maybe you should ask your mother where she has been. Maybe that is who you should be questioning." He was upset and paced some more. We sat at the table and watched him. He was sweating and took some pills. He was hurt. He was upset. I put it all together. My mom was out with someone else, and he didn't like it. Our family was broken. I took Nico up to bed and laid with him until he fell asleep. Then I cried. Dad left, I don't know where he went. Maybe to Briana; he must be living there. But he wasn't living with her— she just wanted the baby and a house. She used him, and he fell for it. He was paying for a family that doesn't want him in Westchester, while our family in the city was in shambles. He was losing Maria. He couldn't take the pain, so he found someone else.

That Christmas it was obvious that our family wasn't a family any longer. I was aware that my mom was having an affair with her boss. I followed her a few nights and saw them together. My dad knew about it and just went to do his own thing with someone else. I was the keeper of our family. I made the meals, worked on homework with Nico, cleaned the house, and did the laundry. My mom pretended that we didn't know. We knew, but we just pretended back. She still decorated the house for Christmas and insisted that we have a big tree. Then when Christmas was over, the Christmas decorations became stale. I was left to clean up the empty apartment where Nico and I lived. Before Valentine's day, my parents broke the news to us that they would be getting a divorce. My dad was upset; my mom was joyous. *When did they fall out of love? How could she be so happy?* They had switched roles.

She introduced us to her lawyer boyfriend, with whom she shortly got engaged. My dad got engaged to his girlfriend. I snuck girls into my room at night while Nico pretended to sleep in the next room and listen through the wall. My mom wanted to move us to New Jersey, but then I'd have to change schools in my senior year. Nico was in school and would have to change schools too. They both left us. My mom broke my heart. I stayed in the apartment with Nico and continued to be the housekeeper. I babysat my baby sister when it was my dad's weekend, and he was busy off with his new fiancé. Briana had what she wanted—a big house in Armonk, weekend babysitters, and a child support check. I had become a single dad at seventeen.

That summer I got Nico a job with me at the beach club. I wanted him to have the same fun I had working there. We partied together and ignored our family life. Nico was slipping in school, but no one cared. So, that summer we partied.

Most days I picked up Jax to head to work as he lived close by the club. That night we were going to a party at someone's house who had a pool.

"Whose house is this again?" I asked Jax as we finished our night and were getting dressed in the locker room.

"Oh yeah, so this chick is a family friend. Her parents moved to Switzerland a few months ago, and she wanted to stay here. So, my parents watch over her. She lives like a block away. Mad cool, she's like a sister to me. You'll like her."

"Alright. Cool. Sounds like fun." I cracked open beers and handed them out. We arrived at the house party that was just a few friends. She had music playing and a cooler full of beers. There was a table of people playing cards already starting the party. I usually had my party mode on when I entered a house, but somehow when we arrived, I felt intimidated by the stares. I didn't know this crew. I was self-conscious of what I was wearing and checked my hair in the reflection of the window. Jax came in and went into the backyard, but I held back. I looked at the crowd and felt intimidated. I was nervous. This is not who I am. I am a party boy—how could I be so uncomfortable? I went out and said a big hello and excused myself to use the bathroom before really meeting everyone. Jax was already at the table; Nico was close behind him. I went back inside the house. It was dark. I was fumbling around the dining room, looking for the bathroom and hoping it was right past the kitchen.

"The bathroom is over there," a voice said from behind me.

I didn't know that anyone was in the house. It was dark. I turned around and could see the shadows of a girl, but I couldn't see her features. She came to me as I was stuck in my tracks. I dropped my jaw.

"I know that voice, I know it!" I said to myself and dismissed it. I couldn't stop staring at her. The awkward silence was weird. I couldn't talk. She put her hand out as she approached me.

"Hi, I'm Blake. Who are you?" I still was in a trance. The awkward silence was killing me. Time stood still. "*Snap out of it, snap out of it,*" I said to myself. I just stared at her. She smiled and broke the silence. My hands were sweaty, so I quickly wiped them on my shorts before shaking her hand. I chuckled. I had no idea today would be the day I would meet the girl in my head. The flowing long blonde hair. The blue eyes. Her smile. I think I closed my eyes to see if she matched the girl in my head. I was so nervous. That was the day I met Blake.

"Yeah, hi. I'm Maximo." I finally got it together to shake her hand.

"Hello, Maximo. Nice to meet you. You are a friend of Jax's, right?"

I was still staring at her. "Yes, right. Jax. My brother Nico is outside. We all work together at the beach club."

"Cool. So, I'm going to get a beer; the bathroom is right there. See you outside."

"Right, yeah, okay." I couldn't get it together and walked in a circle. I didn't listen to a word she said about where the bathroom was. I didn't even need to use the bathroom. I was wasting time.

When I finally found the bathroom, I stared in the mirror and I looked like I had seen a ghost. *"Is it you? Blake, is it you?"* I saw her face in my memory. I couldn't believe I found her. I finally got myself together and was smiling, eager to know more about my mystery woman Blake. I walked outside and saw no one but her. I gazed at her. She sat at the table and was back into the round of cards. She smiled at me. All I could see was her. The crowd looked at me; I didn't see them. I went and moved close to her. She was going to be the one I wanted to conquer that evening and forever.

I got myself into the game but wasn't paying attention. I could not take my eyes off Blake. The drinks got strong; the laughs got louder; the music played songs that we all sang at the top of our lungs. It was one of my favorite evenings of that summer. I kept bumping into her; I flirted with her shamelessly. She giggled and bumped back. At the height of the party, we started to grunge dance, and I attempted to kiss her. I got my courage up to bring my lips to hers. It was quick, but she pulled away. Girls never pulled away from me. Did I have no game? Why doesn't she understand that she was the girl in my head? In my sketches? I tried to kiss her again. I got the same response. She pulled away. I tried to pull her closer, but she squirmed out of my arms. I tried again when we left for the evening. I was confused that she was not as easy as the other girls. She was my dream. "If God put a dream in your heart trust in him. He will make it happen." I heard my mom say to me. I knew that at this moment God was with me and at that moment I put my trust in him.

CHAPTER THIRTEEN

~

Beers, cards, new friends, and her. I met her. My Blake. To touch her lips, I tingle from that last one. I came home and couldn't stop smiling. I had found her! Her name is Blake. I FOUND her. Thank you, God; thank you, God; thank you, God! My family life, my family problems faded away. Nico was finding his own life; I was just his babysitter. I held the paper with her phone number on it next to me as I smiled.

Blake worked at a camp close to the beach club. When I picked up Jax the next morning, I quizzed him about her.

"So, she's really cute. Why doesn't she have a boyfriend? Where does she go to school? Is she our age? Where does she hang out?"

I had so many more questions, but Jax stopped me and laughed. He was moving about in his seat and laughing. I didn't get it, but I started to laugh too.

"What's so funny?" I asked him.

"Dude, you're hysterical! You like her that much? She didn't give you much play. Don't you usually just move on?"

"No, Bro. Like, no girls ever resist me. I mean like I am *the man*." We both laughed. It was obnoxious, but I did like her. She resisted me. That didn't happen often. I was off my game. Jax just laughed even more. I had to admit I was funny. I laughed as well. It showed that I liked her. I had to figure out a game plan to get to see her again.

We had parties for the rest of the summer. I called Blake a few times to hang out. She politely declined, but I was not giving up. Casually I asked Jax about her, and he blew it off. I'm not sure why. He was my best friend. We did everything together. It was as if he didn't want me to be with her even though he didn't like her for himself. They acted like brother and sister. He had a serious girlfriend since last year, so what was the problem?

"So, Jax, are you mad that I like Blake? I know you guys are close."

"Ah no? I, I don't know. You hook up a lot, and that's great, but you always have a new girl. Her friends talk; she knows that about you. She dates, but I know she doesn't do much more than fool around a little. Maybe she thinks you'll push her for more? I don't know. I don't talk to her about you. She's my friend; I don't want her to get hurt. She's like a sister to me, you know that."

"Bro, I don't want to hook up with another girl if I have Blake. I have hooked up with lots of girls in the past, but I don't want to be with another one if I have her. I want to be good to her. I promise." I was serious, and Jax was not reacting. He shrugged as if he didn't feel comfortable talking about her. I had to find a new way to get to Blake.

"Yeah, cool. It's not up to me; it's up to Blake. I believe you; I can believe you will be good to her."

"Alright, thanks." I know I was asking for permission from someone that I don't need permission from, but I needed validation. I needed to get Blake to like me.

Senior year started, and I was distracted by football and trying to get into college. I was like my dad in that I didn't want to have my parents pay my way. I received various scholarships to colleges, and I finally decided on an art school in Rhode Island. The thought of going into finance like my dad wasn't appealing right now. I also wanted to concentrate on getting closer to Blake.

CHAPTER FOURTEEN

~

My mom came home sometimes to see us, and sometimes my dad too. Mom wasn't as happy after time went by with her new fiancé. My dad was depressed but still had another family to attend to. He was spread thin. He still was in love with my mom, and she knew it. I didn't understand their love affair. He wouldn't admit it out loud that he loved her. She was so cold towards him, but there were nights they both conveniently spent in our apartment together. I was so confused by love.

I didn't get to see Blake again until senior year was almost over. Jax invited me to a party at her house; I was so excited. I thought about her; I drew her over and over again in my sketch pad. I called her and left messages; sometimes she called me back. It was a struggle for me. She invited me to her party, and I was excited about seeing her. We arrived a bit early, and I was again nervous to see her. She was just as beautiful as I remembered, maybe even more. I wondered if she was dating someone, where she was going to college, and when could I see her again. When could I kiss her for more than three seconds? I never forgot those seconds.

"Hey, girl, you look lovely. How have you been?" I asked her, trying to be as cool as possible. I walked over to her to give her a kiss, which she politely accepted.

"I'm good, how are you? Sorry I didn't call you back. I've been busy with school and getting ready for college."

I was dying to know where she was going. I could not get much info out of Jax. "Yeah, I know, me too. I'm heading out to Rhode Island for school. How about you?"

"Nice, I am going to go live with my family in Switzerland and go to a school there. I kind of miss them." *How could she go to Switzerland?*

"Switzerland? Wow, okay, nice, nice. I'm a little shocked. We must make sure that we have a good summer together then." I felt my confidence back; I felt I could win her over. *Blake, I am so in love with you, can you feel it?* I chanted in my head, hoping she could feel my energy.

"Yeah, for sure. We'll hang out. I plan on some good parties this summer." She looked at me over her shoulder with a flirty smile. I wanted her so badly.

"Alright," I said very unconvincingly. I had to make this the best summer of our lives. I had to win her over.

The party was soon underway; her usual crew was there. I'm starting to like them; they're very much like Jax and Blake. She was flirty with me, but she flirted with other guys as well. I wasn't sure how to read her signals. We drank and told ridiculous jokes. I became her sidekick when we did stupid skits for a game in the kitchen. We blended together well. When I became just drunk enough and she started to let her guard down, I went in for a kiss. I took her hand and escorted her to the back den. I touched her hips, and she touched my arms. When I pulled her in for a kiss, she didn't pull away this time. I moved my hands to the loops of her jean shorts and pulled her closer to me. I wanted her to feel how excited I was. She groaned. The kiss became harder, and she moved her hands down my back to touch my ass. I did the same back to her.

"Hmm, look at you. A feisty little girl." She pushed me away laughing and went over to the couch. I followed her like the schoolboy that I was and leaned over to her as I tested out the waters of how far she was willing to go. She pulled me on top of her and pushed her hands under my shirt; I worked my way to get into her pants. I didn't get very far.

"Hold off. Not yet," she said while I was still on top of her in defeat.

"Alright, alright." I pushed my way off her as I didn't want to fall into that situation again. Man, she was playing me. She laid there on the couch and watched me trying not to make eye contact. I was embarrassed and wanted more. I needed to regain my composure.

"Maximo, I don't want to move too fast. Come on, let's go back to the party." She took my hand and smiled.

"Alright, Blake. My good girl. Alright," I said as we walked back to the slowly dying out party. The night was waning. I went out and opened another beer and sat in the cold with Jax to have a cigarette.

"So, did you hook up with Blake?" he asked me.

"Yeah, a little. I don't get her, but I really like her, Jax, I do. Does she not like me?" I had lost my confidence again.

"She hooked up with you? Yeah, I think she likes you, man. Don't overthink it. She doesn't go too far with guys. She flirts and dates for sure. But she doesn't go too far with hooking up—that's what I'm told. But, she's cool, so if you like her, take it slowly."

"Alright, bro, that's good advice. I'll take it slow with her."

We punched our beers together and went back inside to find the party was basically over. Jax and his girlfriend left, and I was there alone with Blake. She wasn't kicking me out too fast. We looked at each other from across the kitchen and just smiled. I went over to grab another kiss and not force her to do anything else. She took the gentle kiss that turned into a long session of standing in place. I held my hands on her face to show I was not going to force her to do much more. She caressed my body and teased me as her hands ran across the front of my pants. Oh, it tingled. I was so ready for her, but she wasn't. After the tease, she held her hands on my forearms. We continued to kiss until we needed to stop for air.

I touched my head to her head with my hands still holding her face. We will do this often in our relationship. She was so warm and comfortable. She controlled her breathing while I can't. She helped me calm down, kissing my cheek and giving me a long shush.

"Blake, I don't want to force you to do anything."

"I know you don't."

"I don't want to be away from you."

"I don't want you to leave." She took my hand and escorted me to her bedroom. We didn't do much, but it was the best sleep I had that I could ever remember. She laid in my arms with her head on the inside of my shoulder, my chin tucked over her head. Her snoring was light, and she caressed my arm and down my leg the majority of the night. It was peaceful. With other girls, I would have been cramped by now, still awake from the awkward hold and wanting to leave the situation. With Blake, I didn't care. I was so happy to be with the woman I sketched. I wanted to win her over.

She awoke by moving her head slightly from side to side, and I had to move mine for her to move. She looked up at me with a smile. I smiled back.

"Hey, Pumpkin. Good morning," I sarcastically whispered. She responded with a light slap to my chest. We moved to face each other on our sides, just admiring the nice sleep we had and daydreaming of what more would feel like. I ran my finger down the outside of her cheek, and she leaned into it. I wanted to make her happy. She leaned over for another kiss. Her pull on my lower lip was like a tide going out for the day. She could have pulled as hard as she wanted, I was not letting go. I moved my arm to cuddle her close.

"So that was nice. How about I make you breakfast and help you clean up?" I asked her as I ran my fingers in her hair, hoping to get some strands to hold onto. She was always smiling.

"I would love that. Thank you, Maximo," she said as she leaned in for another kiss and ran off to the next room. I sighed as I moved to lay flat on my back in her bed. I took the brief seconds I had to smell her odor on the sheets and take inventory of what her haven looked like. She had posters on the walls and still had her dollhouse from being a kid. I found a picture of her with her family—they all looked the same. Her younger brother and sister were with their parents at the beach, all in matching outfits. She must have been well trusted to be living alone. Jax's family highly regarded her as a trusted teenager. *Oh, Blake, I can't wait to get to know you. I can't wait to be with you forever.*

CHAPTER FIFTEEN

~

Dad came to stay with us more and more often. He had questions about Mom and was depressed. I didn't ask much about his current relationship; it was obvious that it wasn't working out. He still loved Mom.

"So, do you know how she's doing? When was Maria last here?" He was fishing and desperate.

"I don't know, Dad, why don't you call her?" He smoked his cigarettes in the house. Although I smoked myself, it made me sick to live in the midst of the smoke. I was starting to use cigarettes less and less since Blake didn't smoke. I wanted to be the best for her.

He was upset and depressed. "Yeah, I don't know. She seems happy. She is happy, right? Love is so weird. I really loved her, you know? I really messed up, huh?" Was he asking me if he messed up? Our family was a mess. I did anything I could to avoid them. Nico was now on his own; we rarely crossed paths in the house. I still was the housewife but learned to disappear as often as possible.

Dad went back to his new life and came to terms that his relationship with my mom was over. They were divorced, and he didn't like it. I led two lives. No one knew about my family life—I kept my friends and my family separate. They don't know any of my friends except for Nico. It was becoming easy to push my family aside. My mom basically abandoned us right after my dad left. I didn't want that for my life. My mom and I had a special bond, but she remained distant to us. I missed her. I was having a hard time with that. I dwelled on it from time to time when I came home, and she wasn't around. I didn't hear from her. But at least now I had Blake.

Blake was my favorite dream, my favorite distraction, and I'd find any excuse to bring her up in conversation. It is embarrassing now that I am looking back at it, but I didn't care. I needed her. At my afternoon break from the pool, I raced over to see her even for a quick kiss. I had a serious infatuation. She knew nothing about me or my home life. I didn't want to expose her to it. I also didn't want any of my friends to know about her. Blake and I were at a standstill on our hookups. I was fine with that. I just wanted to be close enough to kiss her, smell her hair, and smile at her. My time was limited; I had to be everything she wanted.

I slept over at her house a few nights a week and cuddled into her. It was the best night's sleep I got all week. Blake woke me up with soft kisses to my nose since that was the best she could reach from her angle. I smiled at the welcoming touch.

"Good morning, my Blake," I said before even opening my eyes. She pushed herself on top of me, and I allowed her to crawl on my shoulder. My eyes were still enjoying the other senses to take in the moment. She mapped out zig zags with her finger across my chest exposed from the open buttoned-down shirt I was still wearing from the night before.

"Maximo, can you get a few days off?" she asked.

"I guess so. What did you have in mind? Are you going to kidnap me and take me somewhere fabulous?" I asked jokingly.

"Well, yeah. Kind of. I mean, you can leave a number for your family to call just in case."

"Bahahaha, really? Well, now I will for sure take off. Any chance to be tied up and in your trunk is still time with you, Pumpkin." Will my family care or notice if I was gone? I turned her around so that I was facing her and had the chance to grab a kiss.

70

"I want to take you to my parent's summer house," she said. "They rent it out for basically the whole year, but they keep it open for a long weekend in July for us. So, since they're in another country, it's mine. I could bring a bunch of friends, but I think I'd rather spend this time alone with you. What do you think?" I was so excited; I wanted nothing more than time alone with Blake.

"Hmm, all that time alone with you? I don't know, Blake. I might not like you by the end of the weekend. Your endless teasing and all..." She smacked me playfully and looked away. I was seriously kidding. But we've been seeing each other for weeks, and it was hard to wait. I had to wait. I will wait for her, but it was killing me. I now hit a nerve and probably lost my chance for the weekend and to have this wish granted. I moved in to kiss her neck, making stupid noises and bites as if I was going to take a real bite into her neck. She could not help but laugh as it tickled her.

"I'm sorry, babe. I know you don't like me. It's alright, no pressure." She let out a gasping laugh that was painful for her.

"I like you so much, Maximo." She didn't look at me.

"Hey, hey." I took my hand to move her face to look at me and readjusted my body to make her comfortable.

"I'm seriously kidding. I want to be with you. Even if you won't let me hold your hand, I just want to be with you. I'm a jerk. I don't know how to be sensitive, but I don't want to hurt you ever. You make me really happy, Blake." She wiped away a tear. She couldn't hide from me. Her face was red. She was embarrassed because she wanted to hear that I was not going to hurt her. I kept smiling at her, and when she was able to control that tear, she kissed me.

CHAPTER SIXTEEN

~

Back into the city. Back to the harsh reality that my family was a mess. I ran home after work to feel out the war zone. Although I wasn't there every day, I was still close enough. Heading to the beach for a few days made me nervous. I still never told Blake about my family. The apartment was silent. I thought I was alone, but I wasn't. As I gathered my clothes to take with me to the wash, I heard movement in my parent's bedroom. The door was opened just enough for me to look in, and I didn't see anyone. I kicked it open to find my mom in the far corner sleeping against the window. I didn't have time for this today. I attended to my laundry with anger. *"You cannot do this to me today. Not today. I want this time with Blake, don't do this to me."* I repeated in my head. I was so angry throwing my clothes around that I didn't hear Mom come into the kitchen.

"Who are you talking to Maxie?" she asked with a smile on her face.

"Oh hi, I didn't know you were here. I'm just talking to myself." I was nervous and confused, so I laughed a bit. "Don't call me Maxie," I demanded. She laughed.

"Oh, okay. So, what are you doing? Are you going to be home tonight?" I could have been, but I didn't want to. We leave in the morning. I wanted to be with Blake.

"No. I'm going away for the weekend, and we leave in the morning. I'm going to spend the night with my friend." I didn't look at her. I just looked at the clothes I was pulling out of the dryer.

"Can you maybe stay here tonight? Since you're leaving in the morning? Nico is coming over, and so is your dad. We want to have dinner as a family. You can leave after dinner if you must."

I was so mad she asked me, but I was not home much. If there was a bombshell coming, I wanted it out in the open before my trip with Blake, so I would not have to wonder about what it was. I could push it away into the closet with all the other family pain.

"Alright," I said. After I folded my clothes, I went into my room to puff off steam.

After some time, Nico came in along with my dad a few minutes later. Mom was cooking. I didn't offer to help since I had been doing most of the cooking the past few years. It was, of course, my dad's favorite pork chops. She was buttering him up for something. Mom called me to the table, and my parents were all smiles and kisses. Nico was now at the same point I was—over it. He was failing in school and didn't care much about anything. We were not the friends we used to be. Our family life separated us.

The dinner finally got underway, and I watched the clock. I wanted to get back to Blake and to the party she was attending. *So where is the bombshell?* I wondered. I wanted to get it this over with.

"So, Dario, Maximo is going to go away for a few days with a friend," my mom said. Nico looked over to me as if I were getting set-up for something.

"Really, Maxie, where are you going? Which friend? Do I know him?" my dad asked.

"Do you know any of my friends? It's my girlfriend. We're going to her summer house for a few days. And PLEASE! Stop calling me Maxie."

"You're right; I don't know most of your friends, Maximo. I hope that we can start over with a new slate. So, with that said, your mom and

I have decided to get back together. We're moving back into the house in Armonk. Briana is getting married and has moved out. We want to start over as a family. Nico, public school will be good for you."

"Are you serious? I'm not leaving my high school during my last year. This sucks!" Nico slammed his fists on the table. It jumped. We all jumped back with it. He stormed into his room to grab something and then left. I took it as my cue to leave too.

"Alright, great thanks for letting me know. So, when I pack up my stuff to go to school, I guess I'm taking everything? Great thanks. Oh, yeah, and Mom? I hope that you're happy with him. Thanks for all the nights I spent with you as you cried over him and couldn't get out of bed. Really worth it. Thanks, guys, you happy lovers." I went into my room, stuffed my bag with my things, and left with the same slam that Nico gave. I was so pissed.

Nico was nowhere in sight, I went to the payphone and paged Blake that I was on my way and drove myself to Westchester. I blasted obnoxious music the whole way. I was so mad and need to make the anger disappear. I channeled all my energy to focus on making Blake happy. I stopped by the gas station to buy her flowers and her favorite beer. No one carded me much; I looked old enough. I got to her house, but it was empty. After I drove around to a few houses, I found them. She was drunk at a party. I was happy for her. She was having fun, but I just wanted her attention and not to party. I had a drink to join the crowd. When I took her home, she was tipsy, and it was funny. I was trying to let my guard down and laugh with her. Tonight, we just were not on the same wavelength. It was my fault. The flowers sat on the kitchen table. She ran over to them to smell them.

"Maximo, are these for me? How did you know?" she said as she opened the plastic and worked on getting them into the water. I stopped her from making a mess and handed her a beer as she sat down in a chair.

"Every beautiful woman deserves flowers, my dear." I smiled at her slumped in her chair. She was so funny when she was drunk.

"It means a lot to me, Maximo. I can't wait to take you to my summer house tomorrow." She was propped up on the table, and when the flowers were in the water back on the table, I carried her up to bed.

CHAPTER SEVENTEEN

~

We left early in the morning to avoid traffic. The day was cloudy, so we wore our jackets. Blake was still sleepy, so I drove and kept the music low until we arrived at the house. Blake awoke with crinkles at the side of her eyes. She was still beautiful. The weather was cloudy, and after we unpacked the car, we went for a walk on the beach.

"You are quiet today, Maximo. Are you okay?" she asked as she kicked sand on me. I was still brooding over my parents. I wasn't sure if I could let her into that part of my life or not.

"I'm alright, just nervous around you." I was deflecting. I kicked a bit of sand on her toes and sped a few steps ahead of her. She could detect that I was not right. We went for lunch on the boardwalk and played some games along the way. We picked up drinks at a bar and walked the rest of the way with our large funnel cups of alcohol and fake juices that gave us drunken Pumpkin rushes. I was still unusually quiet on that cloudy day. We stopped to watch the ocean. The wind picked up, and Blake grabbed my arm to hug for warmth. I watched the ocean and concentrated on the waves and her comfort.

"So, Maximo, when are you going to tell me about your family?" The question I avoided and dreaded to answer. I wanted to lie; I wanted to deflect. I could not lie to my Blake. She was so special to me. I was embarrassed by my family.

"Oh, now what do you want to know about them? I'm the best of the crew. Are you trying to see where Nico is? Huh? Do you think he's cuter than me?" I asked jokingly and gave her a slight push before grabbing her to come into me for a kiss. I chose the deflecting game.

"Now, Maximo, you know I think you are the sexiest. Come on now. I want to know about them. I feel like I talk about my family all the time. I miss them. I want to know about yours because you're important to me. I want to know all about you, Maximo." She nudged at me, but I concentrated on the ocean. She was right. I liked her too. She should know about my family and me. I had to let her in to get closer to her.

"I don't know. They kind of suck. I just don't like to talk about them. My mom and dad split up after my dad cheated on her. She was a mess for a long time. Then my dad had a kid with that woman as my mom had a miscarriage. It was ugly. We lived in Armonk, and then we moved back to the city. My dad came back, my mom cheated on my dad. My dad cheated on her. They got a divorce. He found someone else. My mom moved out with her boyfriend, broke up with her boyfriend, and moved back. My dad broke up with his girl and now they told me we're moving back to Armonk and getting back together. So, I'm kind of angry about it. I just have been taking care of all of them. Then they decide everything is going back to when it was great because we're going to live behind a white picket fence. It's just bullshit. I would never do that to you. I mean if you ever became my wife and all. I mean, not now, like way in the future. Oh, I'm sure you'll get rid of me by then."

"Wow, Maximo. That's a lot to hold in. I wish you told me this before."

"You don't need to know this mess. I'd rather keep it away from you. You always talk about how great your family is and how you miss them and all this fun stuff you do together. In my family we don't even talk. It's just a mess." I kept my eyes on the ocean waves. Blake hung on my arm with her eyes fixated on me. I could feel her. It made me feel good and warm. I started to smile. She nudged me.

"What? What are you looking at?" I nudged back at her, and she signaled to come in closer for a kiss.

"Maximo, I like you so much right now. You have no idea." We kissed again. I felt safe and warm.

That evening we went back to the house that looked over a small lake on the other side of the ocean. Blake picked up lobsters and some wine. She insisted I sit on the porch and have a cocktail as she put dinner together. The weather was breaking, and the sun was setting. It was relaxing. She played our favorite grunge tapes and sang along. It made me sing along with her in a light whisper. I felt so at ease. I was so happy that I told her my story, and she didn't run. I felt accepted and loved. *Wow,* I thought, *love. I think I've finally admitted that I'm in love with Blake. I'm so in love.*

We ate on the back porch with candles. Fireworks burst in the sky from time to time. The fourth of July had already passed, so they must have been just for fun. We got silly from our wine. I took her to sit on the outdoor couch and lay by me. It was beautiful, hearing the dings from the boats, the sound of people in the streets, and the ocean waves behind us. She smelled so beautiful, and I took sniffs of her hair as I got looser from the wine. It was a perfect evening.

"So, Blake, why do you come out this weekend every year? Is it like your parents' anniversary or something?"

"Or something."

"Oh, so I get to tell you my family secrets, but I can't know yours? Shady..." I kissed the side of her head.

"It's alright, Blake. I still love you anyway." I said it; I put it out there.

"Really? Do you love me? Is it the wine talking?"

"Nope, the lobster I just ate. He isn't dead. He wants to get out. I think he's trying to win over your heart. It's a ploy."

"You know, I didn't cook him on purpose. You know, lobsters mate for life. So, mine is alive too." Blake played off my sarcasm so well.

"Mate, huh? I'd like to know more about that. How is that done again?" I poked at her as she screamed out in laughter. She turned to me and stood up grabbing my hand to stand up. She pushed herself into my body and ran her fingers down my chest into my pants. I braced not to attack her and gave her breasts the gentle touch. She was so delicate. I don't want to hurt her.

"I don't know. You will have to show me." She smiled and kissed me again.

"Yeah? Are you sure? I don't want to disappoint you and all. Maybe I don't know how?"

"Maximo, you will never disappoint me." She took me to the bedroom and pushed me onto the center of the bed and undressed slowly for me. She took care of me. I let her do what she wanted and lead the way. It was simple but so meaningful. I'm not sure if it was her first time or not, but she knew what she was doing. I didn't want to have sex with another woman after that. I hope that I wouldn't have to. When it was over, she wrapped herself into a sheet and me into one. We went out onto the back porch and drank more wine. It was a magical evening for both of us. She made me feel warm and loved. I had my Blake wish. It was everything.

"So, Blake... Stop avoiding the question. Why do you come out this weekend every year?" I picked up the conversation again.

"Because, because. It's my birthday. I always love to spend it at the beach. Now, I will always want to spend it at the beach with you. I'm falling in love with you, Maximo."

"I'm glad that I gave it up to you then," I said. We both laughed. I pulled her in for a long kissing session and another session of sex that was a little less vanilla than the first, second, and third time around. I had for sure fallen for Blake. When she fell asleep on my chest, I brushed back her hair and whispered in her ear. "I love you, Blake. I love you more than you know." I thanked God that night for giving me this promise of Blake.

CHAPTER EIGHTEEN

~

Blake went off to Switzerland, and I went up to college. I put my sappy parents behind me as they moved out of the city and back to Armonk. I had a chance to drown in my creative side. I never showed Blake the sketches of her. They were so vulnerable. But I know that one day I will.

I was alright with her so far away. She sent me postcards all the time, and I sent her some too. We kept it light and promised to talk on the phone from time to time. We gave each other permission to meet and date other people. It was a reassurance that we wanted to be together and be the best we could be for each other. But if someone had strong feelings for another, we had to share it right away. We had a pact. The girls up here were artsy, not like the preppy bitches from back home. Certainly nothing like my Blake. Yup, I just called Blake a preppy bitch. She knows it.

I found a crowd I wanted to avoid. But I found them. I'm not a person that can drown in my creativity. So, I found the guys who partied, smoked pot, and drank. We listed to endless *Tribe Called Quest,* and any music that went well with the pot. I didn't have to study hard; I had to be creative. The girls there were hippies; I wasn't interested. I did still love Blake. She was my everything. But I know I promised to live my life. I know she was too. I hoped there was no one out there better for her than me. I knew there couldn't be.

The time there was easy. Being creative made me silly, and the seriousness of life was left at home in Armonk. That wasn't my home. I was smoking pot every day, because the guys in my house were selling, I started to as well. It was a way to meet girls. They would do anything for some if they didn't have money. I was getting girls left and right. I didn't even have to try. We sold before class, after class. The school was aware it was going on, but they put a blind eye to it. Or at least we were getting away with it. The campus police came by from time to time and confiscated some stuff. We got written up, but what did it really mean? I also worked at a local burger place in town for money. I was living in a college fantasy. This place was too easy. It was a distraction away from Blake. How was she doing in college? We spoke from time to time. I called her drunk or stoned all hours of the day. She giggled. Those calls were short. Then we had days when the calls were longer: When she needed comfort through exams or when I needed to just hear her voice. She was very serious about schoolwork whereas I was having the time of my life partying and not having to worry about hard work. School was just easy for me. She was in school for business and had a hard workload. She didn't party as much, but she did get out there. She told me about boys she was dating or just having fun with and then made sure I knew she wanted to be with no one else other than me. I needed to hear that. We kept up with letters and postcards. Her family was taking her traveling at the beginning of the summer. Then she was going to do volunteer charity work. Oh, how opposite we were!

I worked the weekends at the burger joint in town. I really didn't need the money but I needed the sanity of it. It turned out to be a great place to sell weed too. The guys had a ring going where we split up the areas. I had sales coming to the counter and even under the cameras I was able to make a sale through napkins and empty burger boxes. Little did I know I was being set up. I had someone I didn't know come and order the "pepperoni pizza with a small coke." Then I would reply with, "Oh you mean the burger special maybe?" "Yeah that one," they'd say. I charged for the burger, placed the stash in the box, the real payment in the register, and the guy one-handed it back to me in a napkin. It worked. I was so proud of myself. But when the customer I didn't know was an undercover cop, I was caught. I was handcuffed and sent to jail. It was my first offense, but I had a record on campus that was not favorable. I spent that night in jail. No one came to bail me out. When I got out in the morning and walked home, the house was celebrating. They had made a big sale. They set me up to get caught so they could make the big deal without a hitch. I thought they were my friends. At close to the end of the year, I moved out. I never sold drugs again. I transferred to NYU as my parents were alumni there. It made it easier for me to transfer and hold my art credits. I also decided that maybe my dad was right. Finance was better for me. So with the transfer home, I became a business major and never learned more about art again.

That summer was boring to me. I went to the parties; I worked at the beach club; I drove by Blake's house that was rented to a family. I sat in the front sometimes and pictured Blake coming out waving her hair. She didn't keep me waiting, but she made an entrance. She wasn't coming out today. *"Oh, my Blake, my Blake, I will wait for you."* I sped off and went to the unpleasant home in Armonk.

CHAPTER NINETEEN

~

Fall came in just the right time. I needed a new distraction and to get out of the house. My parents acting like we were a perfect family was nauseating. If it made them happy, then great. Nico and I didn't buy it. I wanted to believe in love, but their love seemed fake. How could my mom love someone who had hurt her so badly? I can't imagine doing that to Blake.

I stayed in the dorms, and the workload was easy for me. I distracted myself with hanging in the local bars and parties. There were girls, lots of girls. They were meaningless to me. I was a pawn of sorts; I didn't care. I was using them right back. I always thought of Blake. Through these years we talked less and less. The phone calls were still me drunk reaching out to her, then there were the long calls that had meaning. She had a boyfriend; I was okay with that. She told me she wasn't in love with him but wanted to experience someone else while we were apart. I decided to get a girlfriend myself for the same reasons. We both believed it would allow us to grow; and when we could be together, it would be like the first time all over again. I went through the motions, but there was no one I wanted more than Blake.

My dad got me a low-end job at a bank after graduation, and I was to work my way up the ranks as he said it would mold me. Whatever. It was easy; it was fun. I was a gofer basically, but I had fun with it. I was able to play the charm that I had used at the beach club. Same thing, hotter women who played the stock market that made them even hotter. I thought of

Blake, but she was fading from my memory. I moved into the city, which made my vision of Blake fade more. The temptations, the alcohol, the sex, the women who wanted to have sex in conference rooms when no one was looking all became my life. My identity had changed. I was a bank zombie. The popularity got me promoted into sales jobs. I partied with clients, dazzled them at Rangers' games that turned into Yankee games, Giants games, Pearl Jam concerts. My life was one big party that I was getting paid for. Who wanted anything else? I wanted Blake, but suddenly, she became a blur in my vision. I pushed her to the back of my memory. But she was always there. *Blake, I want to be with you. You are with someone else, somewhere else. Don't be mad at me. I don't know who I am without you. I am lost, Blake,* I said to myself some nights. It was hard to live this life, although I made it look so glamorous.

After a few years, the excitement wore off. I started to see how my dad fell in love with this life and how coming home to us was a chore. I went home some weekends to see the family and realized my mom was pushing away from my dad because he was getting bored. It was a hard world to run away from. There were temptations, but the love was always there. The drug of the other was strong. It was hard to resist. I want to be over this life before I get to Blake. I don't want this for us. I want us to be a happy family. We met a few times at her quick stops in New York. I went to Switzerland to see her, but her schedule was always demanding, so the encounters were quick. The sparkle was still there, but the time and dedication at the moment just weren't. I left each time with "Blake, I'm never letting go of you. I won't give up." She smiled and said, "Maximo, it is always you. Don't forget that." It held me through to the next encounter.

CHAPTER TWENTY

~

I met Jacinda one morning as I was leaving for work, and she was on her way for a run. We lived on the same floor. I never noticed her before. She was from Australia. Her smile was big and always very pleasant. Our morning encounters became having coffee together; then I started to also run with her before work. My work life was so boring to me. I went through the motions but held back on the drugs and drinking. At twenty-eight I was becoming too old for the job. Jacinda became my date to events; she suddenly was my companion. She moved in from down the hall, and we became a couple. I liked her; I liked her a lot. I told her I couldn't make a commitment. I never said why. She believed she could convince me otherwise. I never told her I was waiting for Blake. The obvious answer that my parents' marriage was a mess kind of sent the message.

Jacinda and I had a routine; it was nice and calming. We had dinner on Monday nights. Met with friends on Tuesday. Drinks after work on Wednesday. The routine was set. We went to parties, work functions. She was my partner. The only problem was, I wasn't in love with her. She was just a wonderfully beautiful woman on my arm. She wasn't Blake.

Eventually, my parents split up again. Dad moved out and found someone else. Mom stayed in the house and fell into a depression. I went to stay with her a few nights a week. Nico was in and out, mostly out. I fed her, made sure she showered, cleaned the house, and grocery shopped for food. I even laid next to her at night. I got out my sketch pad again and drew. Jacinda didn't know where I was. I was again hiding my family because I didn't want anyone to know. My mom asked about her, and I dismissed it.

"I love you, Maximo; I love you more than you know," she'd say to me when I came over.

"I know, Mom; I love you too. Please get better, Mom. You shouldn't live like this; it's crazy!"

"I know, Maximo. Love is hard. I did love him."

"Yes, and he hurt you, and you went back to him. But I do know that he loved you too."

"I know he did. We can't hold it together. Go hold it together. Go get that girl you draw. Did you find her yet?"

"Yes, I found her."

"Good, so where is she? Is she the girl you are with now?"

"No, I'm not with her now. I miss her every day. She's in Switzerland; she has a boyfriend. It's okay. We'll be together."

"I can see it, Maximo; I can. You have her in your heart as I had you in mine. Go and find her."

"Yes, Momma. I will." I gave her a kiss and went home to sneak into my apartment and back to Jacinda who pretended to not be awake. I fell straight asleep. I had Blake on my mind. I had called her before I left the house, and it went straight to voicemail. I couldn't leave a message. I didn't want to upset her. As I was fast asleep, Blake came into my vision. When I saw her face, she was so beautiful. I knew I was smiling in my sleep. It was as if I were sitting next to her. She was with her family at night, driving and singing in the car. They were a happy family. I didn't know what that felt like. It was a dream that felt real.

Then my mind went back to my mom in bed. She was crying, but then she was smiling. She walked about the house looking for things to remember us by. I was glad to see her feeling good about memories. She made me smile. Then my dream was blank. I was asleep. There was darkness. I was peaceful. I saw Blake again, laughing and her hair in the wind.

They were still in the car driving home from a dinner they shared. She was smiling and looking at me. I felt her. Then there was darkness. A truck came from the divider and went straight into their car. It crashed, spun around, and then was slammed again by the truck and other cars. They were now in an accordion. Her parents were instantly dead, and the same with her brother and sister. Then there was Blake. She was bloody, her mouth dripped blood. I couldn't save her. I couldn't see her body.

"Maximo, Maximo. Talk to me. Keep me alive, Maximo. It is you I have in my heart. Keep me alive, Maximo. I want to see you again. I want to have a family with you. Maximo, keep me alive. Just talk to me until help gets here. Please."

"Blake, Blake, my love. Stay with me now. You can't die. You have to stay alive; stay with me. Blake, I will take care of you. Come to me; find me. I'll be waiting for you. Blake, you will be okay. I love you so much, Blake; I hope that it can be enough to keep you alive. Blake, I love you, stay with me!"

The paramedics came and took her out of the car. "It was amazing that she's still alive!" the paramedics said in shock.

"Blake, I love you!" She was taken away. I was screaming to her in my sleep.

"Maximo, I love you, your love kept me alive. I am in good hands now." I watched the ambulance take her away. At her words, a white cloud came over me. I was at peace now that Blake was safe. The dream was off to another piece of my conscious. I was relaxed and smiling. "I love you so much, Blake."

And with that, I was woken up by Jacinda. My dream was real; I just knew it. Jacinda was not happy; I had some explaining to do.

"So that is where you go at night? Blake? Really Maximo? I should have known you were never going to propose. You are a horrible person, Maximo!!" She took her stuff and left. I never saw her again. She didn't even give me a chance to explain. I didn't want to. I told her I was never going to make a commitment. She didn't want to believe me. She wanted to think she could make me love her over the woman in my heart. No one can break that love.

I spent the next few weeks with my mom who was gradually getting better. I tried to call Blake over and over again. No answer. Is she okay? No opportunity to leave a voicemail, the box was full.

"Blake, I love you. Please tell me you are okay," I said out loud. I closed my eyes and saw her in a hospital bed. *"I am okay, Maximo; I am okay. I love you, Maximo."* Then the moment would fade away again in my mind. She was okay—that was all I needed to know.

CHAPTER TWENTY-ONE

~

I was making breakfast, and my mom came out from her room with a packed bag. I stopped in my tracks.

"Maximo, I don't know how to tell you this. I'm going to go and live in Miami. I have a bunch of friends there. I need to leave New York and start over."

"What? What do you mean you're going to Miami? What about your job? Your life here?"

"Maximo, you are my life. Nico is my life. You are both grown up and don't need me anymore. You don't want to live here. You don't live here! You have a place in the city. Go and be there. Go be with the girl you sketch. Give me grandchildren. Don't waste your life. I don't want to stand in your way. You're heartbroken and taking care of me to help you feel better. I'm going." She came over to me with a kiss to my forehead and to steal some bacon.

"At least stay and have breakfast," I said. I needed her. She was right. I was hiding behind her to mask the pain of not knowing where Blake was and the fact my girlfriend left me last year. Now I was lost. I lost touch with my friends and scaled back at work. I needed to move on.

"I'm going now, Maximo. I'll call you. Let your father worry about the house and go back to the city." She left, and I was there with a plate of bacon that I sat and ate. I was overeating, over drinking. I was a mess. I left with a packed bag, and after work went back to my apartment that felt so empty. I tried to call Blake again. No answer; I left a message. I have been leaving messages. I checked my mail to find an invite to Jax's wedding. I hadn't spoken to him in years. Will Blake be there? I couldn't wait to find out. I sent in my RSVP immediately and got myself into the gym. I wanted to look perfect for her.

At work, I was becoming more of the behind-the-scenes person instead of the frontman. It was an adjustment, and for now, I was fine with it. The brokers needing to put in info always bribed me; the woman for sure flirted heavy. They were a perfect distraction. I flirted back; I wanted to get back into my game. I was working out again, eating better, and getting back into shape. I never stopped picturing seeing Blake in a few weeks. But this distraction of losing Jacinda, losing my mom, and not being able to find Blake was grating on me.

Barbara was an older woman, still attractive. Her husband left her a few years earlier. She always flirted hard with me. She was a senior manager on my team so I worked under her. Whatever she asked I did. They called the shots; my team just did as they were told. What was the harm? She took me to dinner a few times to thank me. It was more of an obligation than something I wanted to do. But even though I got back into the game, I was still lonely and depressed. She ran her foot up my leg and reached over to grab me under the table. I was shocked. I didn't move. I was being molested in public. One would think I would like it, but I didn't. She signaled me to the bathroom, and I declined. She signaled again; I declined as politely as possible. She came over to whisper in my ear.

"I think it is in your best interest to meet me in the bathroom. We wouldn't want your commissions to get lost, now would we?" It was blackmail. I didn't know what to do. I was so embarrassed that this was happening. How would I know? I was set up. How do I get out of this? She signaled me again. I whipped my face with my napkin, and out of weakness, I went into the bathroom with Barbara.

She pushed me against the door and locked it. Her hands opened my pants. I stood there. I didn't even touch her unless I had to. She was good;

I will admit that. But I was disgusted by this act. I closed my eyes and saw Blake disappointed in me, my mom disappointed in me. Barbara was proud of herself. I grabbed my pants to pull them up right away.

"I hope you enjoyed yourself, Maximo," she said as she was leaving.

"Great, thanks. I appreciate it. Really. It was good; I just am not feeling well. I'm going to call it a night." I raced out of that restaurant as fast as I could and went home to throw up. I took myself into the shower and wept.

"Blake, I am so embarrassed. Please forgive me. Please. What do I do now?"

I heard no response in my head. I went to bed and tried to erase the ugly memory from my mind.

CHAPTER TWENTY-TWO

~

It was Jax's wedding day. I was so nervous. *"Blake, Blake, will you be there? Do you miss me as much as I miss you?"* I asked myself the whole day in my head. I was back in shape; I was feeling good. All the hurt and bad was behind me. Nothing would stop me from seeing Blake and starting my life with her; I was ready. I hope that she was too.

I think it took me about an hour to shave and another hour to make sure my hair was perfect. My suit was steamed out. I did that the second I got into the hotel room. Jax's fiancé was from Montana, and therefore that was where the wedding was held. I didn't get a chance to talk to him; it had been some time. But I was ready to see Blake.

I arrived a bit late to the cocktail hour as I didn't want to seem so anxious to be looking around for Blake. I ran into old friends and drank scotch to ease my nerves. I could not help but look around. The crowd got thicker. I wandered from conversation to conversation. I wasn't listening. I went to the restroom to check my hair again and calm my nerves, trying to breathe deeply. Blake always helped me breathe deep.

When I walked outside, I saw a blonde at the coat check dropping off her things. It was Blake. I stood by the entranceway to the cocktail party and with my stupid goofy grin on I waited. She was frazzled walking in late. I know that she always wanted to be on time. I was intercepted by someone who turned my focus away. I was trying to be polite, but my friend was tipsy and adamant that I engage in this conversation.

I watched Blake walk by. How did she not catch onto my presence? She made her way over to Jax and his wife and was speaking to some people and shaking hands. I watched her. When the conversation was over through the crowd, I saw Blake at the bar awaiting a drink. Her friends around her, she seemed uninterested as if she never met them before. I could not see anything but her in that room. She caught my eye as I made a beeline to her through the sea of people. She smiled then turned her body to look to the side away from everyone. She was nervous. I went right next to her at the bar and waited for her to say something. She looked and smiled, then looked at the bar with her drink in her hand.

"Uh, hello?" I said sarcastically. She turned to me.

"Hello?" she said and looked at me like she never saw me before. I was upset. She still smiled, maybe she was playing a game. Playing hard to get.

"Blake, come on. It has been forever. I've missed you." I leaned in to grab her for a kiss. I reached for her side, and she flinched and shrugged me away.

"I'm sorry, I..."

"Blake, what now? You're playing hard to get? Like you don't know me? Alright, little lady. I know how you like to role-play. I'll go along with it." She smiled and whatever she was about to say she forgot and sat there and blushed.

"Alright then," she said and walked away from me. I stood in amazement. *That woman drives me crazy; I miss her so.*

I watched her move through her friends as they tried to get her attention, but she didn't recognize their acknowledgments. She retreated to a table with Jax's mom and sat with her until the dinner was about to begin. She had become shy and reserved. *Is that what they are like in Switzerland? Could it change her personality?* My Blake was fun and crazy. Danced until dawn, did shots of vodka. Outspoken, put me in my place. Told jokes, had sarcasm that even kept me on my toes. She always challenged me to be a better person. Who is this Blake here tonight?

I sat at her table and found that she was being blocked by two other girlfriends that also danced around her new personality. I felt as if I was watching her like a hawk. Each time she caught eyes with me she smiled and turned red. I was winning her over. I tried so hard to get into their conversation, but they were blocking me as much as they could. I guess they are all in on this game.

When dinner was over, I got the nerve to ask her to dance. It was an opportunity to get her alone for a few moments. I escorted her to the dance floor. She was nervous. How could she be nervous around me? Well, it has been some time. It has been so many years since we saw each other. Maybe she was afraid I changed? That I didn't like her anymore? *"Oh Blake, I still love you."* I didn't have the nerve to say out loud. I was still trying to play the game.

"Alright, Blake, this is fun and all. So, can we just get back to being us?"

She smiled. "Okay, right. Sure, us. Who is us again? Tell me more. I'd like to know." She was acting shy. It was cute. She held her hands on my neck like we were at an eighth-grade dance. I became nervous too.

"When I see you, I melt. We are the life of the party. I can't sleep without you in my arms. You challenge me to be a better person. I see my future with you, Blake, I always have. We share jokes; you laugh at all my stupid ones. I envision our kids to be crazy like us. I wouldn't want to have it any other way. They would look like you, of course. I am a goofy mess. I love the way you look at me, the way you arouse me and take care of me. No one can give it to me like you can. Blake, I don't want to play this game anymore. I don't want to live without you anymore. I want you back in my life starting now."

I gave my guts out on the table. She pulled in close to me to feel my chest. I think I felt her cry a bit. She leaned her head on my chest, and we danced in silence. I think I shed a tear myself. I missed my Blake.

"Thank you, Maximo. Thank you for this." She excused herself and with the red face that matched mine she ran off to the bathroom. Her friends ran after her. I ran after her and her friend asked me to give her a minute. I went over to the guy at my table and sat in awe of what had just happened. I wasn't sure.

"So, I have no idea what just happened with Blake. But damn. I still love that woman."

"Awesome. That's great. She remembered you?" he asked me excited that there was a revelation.

"Remember me? Oh, yeah dude, that game is over. Come on. I know she was joking."

"Dude, seriously? You don't know? You thought this was a joke?"

"Uh. . .now I don't?"

"No. She was in this horrific accident. Lost her whole family. She was the only one that made it out alive. She has no memory. She doesn't remember any of us. Jax's family has been her only family now. She and my girlfriend have been trying to jog her memory. It's been really hard for her. So, she remembers you? That's serious stuff!"

Wow, wait. I had a dream that she was in an accident. That wasn't a dream? That was real? OMG. OMG. Now I know why she didn't call me back. She didn't know who I was. I was screaming at myself in my head.

"Yeah, she doesn't want to do that memory thing and look at pictures and stuff. Too painful to remember her family. She just wanted to start over." I got up to go and stand by the bathroom and wait for her to come out. Her friends came out first one by one. "Is she okay? I swear, I just found out. I didn't know." I said apologizing for something I didn't do.

"I know you didn't. She asked us not to tell you. She's fine, just overwhelmed. She'll be out in a minute. You're awesome, Maximo. Makes me believe in true love," she said as she grabbed my arm. My tears built up behind my red face. Blake came out of the bathroom.

"Hey, girl. I'm sorry. I didn't know. I really didn't." She started to laugh a tired laugh to break the ice. She came to me for a hug. It was warming.

"I know you didn't. I'm having a hard time with this. I have had people use me because I don't remember or know things. I just want to start over. But you are very charming. I can see how I could have liked you." She was genuine. I was so freaked out that she didn't remember anything. *How do I handle this?*

"Blake, why don't we go for a walk on the deck. Here, take my jacket. It's cool out." We walked on the deck, and I held her close in my jacket to keep her warm. My mind was racing with emotions. I was so selfish to think about myself. I knew in my heart about the accident. *That dream was real, why didn't I do more?* My mind would not stop.

"Maximo, are you okay? I can feel your energy."

"Really, see. I told you we're in sync. Haha." I always try not to be so serious.

"Since my accident, I learn about people by their energies. I really don't remember much other than stuff from childhood. I have to trust my gut on people if they are being real and kind to me. I for sure have my guard up."

"Oh, I can understand that. So, how is my energy? Am I doing okay? Genuine?"

"I think you're funny and adorable. You were so nervous when you came over to me at the bar. I saw you find me and then you glowed. It was as if you saw no one else in the room other than me. I felt special, and I didn't even know who you were. I want to feel that special again."

"Well then. I guess that's settled. We had a lot of heavy energy right here. Why don't we go back to the party and just have fun? Let loose. Let me show you my charm and how you are my favorite sidekick. What do you think?"

"I haven't let loose in some time. I'm having fun with you. Yes, okay. I'm in. But first, Maximo?"

"Yes, Blake?' I replied and looked into her eyes leaning in. She grabbed me for a kiss and then pushed me off.

"I just wanted to know what that felt like." She walked off, grabbing my tie to follow her like her slave. My Blake is back.

We danced all night. I treated her like she was the special guest star. We did shots. We danced like idiots. I flirted like a fool, and she laughed and smiled. All our friends joined in. We created new memories for Blake. It was just like old times. Blake had fun; she was relaxed. I did my job.

We walked back to the hotel, and since Blake had not checked in yet, I carried her suitcase and brought her to the front desk. We were drunk; they did not enjoy us being there. She gave her name, holding up her credit card, and they did not have her in the system. There was no room for Blake.

"Oh man. I canceled it because I wasn't going to come. Ugh! Really no rooms left? What am I going to do?" She sat on the floor and the front desk clerk was agitated. The associate gave me a look to take her away before they called security.

"Alright, Blake. Don't worry. Listen. I know your situation. I know we're starting over here, but I have a room. We're both exhausted; come and stay with me. I PROMISE I won't try anything. I will even stay in these clothes. I can sleep on the floor if you want. Just stay with me. I also don't want to lose another moment with you."

The silence was brutal. I reached out my hand to her, and she took it. I carried her suitcase and held her up to walk to my room. We kissed and I kept away from touching her too much. I wanted to keep my promise. She got comfortable and signaled me to snuggle with her. I did. We found our spot again even though she didn't know that we had one. I missed smelling her hair and holding her.

"Maximo…"

"Yes, my love…"

"I really needed tonight. Thank you for finding me."

"Blake, I will follow you forever." She held my hand a bit tighter. We both had the best sleep we missed for so many years. "My Blake, I love you so much," I whispered in her ear when she was fast asleep.

The morning came along fast. We only had a few hours. My flight was early—an eight-thirty am flight to Atlanta and then La Guardia. My alarm sounded, and I quickly shut it off. Blake opened her eyes and tried to get up. I shushed her back to close her eyes.

"Maximo, I think you said you have an early flight. Don't you need to get up?" She put her head by my neck and talked through my chest.

"Don't worry, Blake; I'll take a later flight. When is yours?" I asked, also with my eyes closed and not wanting to move.

"I'm staying for the brunch, then my flight is in the later afternoon or early evening. I think like six pm."

"Oh, look at you. Well, then, I will switch to your flight."

"Are you sure? I'm going to Chicago. I'm staying there for a bit. I also believe there is a snowstorm on the way back to New York. Do you maybe want to call or try to make this flight?" She was so concerned and looking out for me. Another dozen reasons why I can't let go of my Blake.

"Chicago? What? I didn't think of the late brunch. Alright, anytime I have to spend with Blake, I'm in. I will fly stand-by; it will be fine." I was nervous I might never make it back. But I had no problem missing work if I was spending time with my Blake.

"Maximo, I'm sorry. I don't remember what you do. But what if you can't get back in time for work?

"Oh, Blake. Maybe I will get stuck in Chicago with you. Will you be okay with that?" I did have to get to work. I had taken time off to help with my mom; it may not look good for me. But I wanted to stay with Blake. I couldn't lose this moment. I was so in the moment with Blake.

"You can come to Chicago, but I have to work. So, you'll be bored. Go home to New York. Don't sacrifice your job."

"Yes, my Blake." I squeezed her and we both dozed off for another hour or so.

CHAPTER TWENTY-THREE

~

Blake's alarm went off after some time, and I awoke again with her in my arms. I turned it off, hoping that she didn't hear it, but she had.

"Maximo, what time is it?" she asked, trying to snatch her phone from my hand. We wrestled a bit for it until she grabbed it and gave me her "you are forgiven" eyes. She opened her phone to see it was ten am.

"Okay, cool. Sometime before the brunch this afternoon." She looked at me. I could not resist coming in for another kiss. She was not holding back on one either. I decided to become daring to Blake, as we are still in most of our clothes from the night before. I stood up and took off all my clothes in front of her as she sat up.

"Alright, little lady. I'm going to take a shower. I mean I could always use some company if you want to join me…or not. No obligation." I confidently turned around, heading to turn on the shower and taking my time in hopes she was about to join me. No show. I entered the water as it started to warm up and decided that if I sang loud enough, it would taunt her to come in. She didn't. It was about five minutes and no noise or peaks from Blake. I was intrigued and came out of the bathroom all wet to find an empty room. She was no longer there. "Blake?" I said and there was no response. The door was closed. She had fled the scene. I was crushed.

I took myself back into the shower and turned the hot water a little hotter and then slightly hotter still. It was tolerable, but it hurt. I wanted to feel something. I only knew pain. *"Where did I go wrong, where did I go wrong?"* I asked myself as the heat started to set in. The tears from missing Blake, not the heat, came to surface. *"She's gone, lost. You lost her. How did you lose her? You failed."*

The pain was setting in from not understanding what went wrong. My heart was broken. The heat was turning my skin red; I was enjoying the pain just enough before it got too hot. Just enough. The steam was strong; I could not see anything. Turning it off, I sat down on the tub ledge with my feet up; I could not take the pain further. I was panting enough from the steam.

"Maximo? Maximo?" I heard the door open. Blake came back. She came back! I had to get myself together. I turned the water to as cold as possible. My red blotched body got up and headed to the bathroom door that she already entered with coffee and some breakfast snacks. She was in my shirt all tied up to make herself look cute and grabbed us coffees from the lobby. The steam from the shower helped.

"Hey, girl, you missed a great shower." I once again tried to sway away from my feelings. I hope I didn't look as if I was crying. Because I was.

"Damn, Maximo, it's hot in here. Seriously! I guess you're right you like it hot. Haha," she said and grabbed a towel to wrap me in. I took in her cold skin on this hug.

"I brought you some coffee and a few things to nosh before brunch. Are you okay, Maximo? You seem so hot and red." I kept her in a hug to gather thoughts.

"Yeah, I was trying to create a steam shower since you're afraid to show me some skin. It got hot in there, woo!" She laughed.

"Oh, I'm not shy, Maximo." She looked at me; we kissed. I pulled her close; she was releasing her energy and giving in to me. That morning I was able to get a bit closer than the night before. Her body had become curvier than when we were kids. Imagine that, the last time I was with

Blake I was a kid. I don't care how many years have passed by; I always missed Blake.

After an amazing morning together, she made sure I had proper moisturization for my red blotchy skin. Maybe it was in the stars for me to almost burn myself.

We entered the brunch as a couple and flirted shamelessly at the table. Blake let me keep my hand on her knee. It was the moment I dreamed of. Before we knew it, the brunch was over; we were tipsy from champagne. It was time to head to the airport. The weather in Montana was cold; it was expected. I didn't listen to Blake, the weather in New York was horrible. Snow blizzard. No planes were landing today.

I checked the flights to Chicago and then New York. Maybe I could work out of the Chicago office for a day or two? No flights. All flights booked; the rest canceled. I was stuck in Montana. Blake's flight was about to board, and I had to say goodbye. I hate goodbyes, especially with Blake.

"Blake, this was amazing to connect with you here. When do I get the pleasure of seeing you again? I don't know how long I can wait." I said, kissing her to persuade her to answer.

"Maximo, I'm going to be settling affairs from my parent's businesses they have in Chicago for the next few months before I go back to New York. There's just so much that I need to learn and absorb. It's hard to know who to trust and what I need to do. I'm kind of overwhelmed."

"I can't imagine Blake what you are going through. I want to be with you and help you. I just want to be with you. I'm trying to be genuine. I really miss you; I hope you can see that." I was desperate. I haven't felt like this in front of a girl. I never worried about Blake until now. I want to see her again.

"Maximo, you are from what I can tell being genuine. I can't make a commitment. I'm still trying to understand who I am right now. I do like you, Maximo, and I do want to see you again. So, if you want to come and visit me in Chicago, I would welcome that. Here's my number." She gave me her number. Blake became an adult when I was still an old kid. I didn't see how much she had on her plate and how difficult this was for her. But she gave me her number and asked me to visit her. Our story was not over.

CHAPTER TWENTY-FOUR

~

I stayed in the airport and aimlessly wandered around the terminals. I was on standby to anywhere that could get me closer to New York. That destination was apparently nowhere. I had to call my job and let them know I would not make it for the Monday start. This was not highly regarded, especially with me. I was slipping at work. I was taking care of my mom and moving her to Miami. Coming in late, leaving early. It was noticeable. I made sure my team was on top of their work, but my mind was not all that present. Now I was away at a wedding all weekend, and of course, it looked like I was blowing off work.

I found a bar to dwell in as I watched the screen of canceled fights add additional ones. I may never leave. I decided after a beer to call Blake. She should have landed by now.

"Hi Blake, it's me. Maximo. The man you forgot about. I am still at the airport, no sign of when I will be leaving. Just letting you know. Call me when you get in." Message left. Another beer ordered. Another screen full of flights canceled. No answer back from Blake. I was lost in waiting for her to call me. I stared at the phone and no response. What went wrong? My anxiety was eating me. I called my mom in Miami.

"Hi Mom, just checking in. I'm stuck at the airport since I missed my flight this morning. So yeah. I probably won't make it home for tomorrow. Hope that you're having a good day. Alright, talk to you later." Message left. Another beer ordered. Flights are starting to come back up on the board. I went to check as soon as I finished and got myself onto a flight to Denver. It was a start. It was something new to do.

I arrived in Denver after midnight and decided to call Blake again.

"Hey, girl. It's Maximo. I made it to Denver. Next flight to New York is at six am. I promise I'll make it this time. Did you make it home? Making sure you're okay. I can't wait to see you again. Alright, call me." Message left. I found a spot at the gate, propped up my bag, and did my best to fall asleep.

The flight was on time; I freshen up in the bathroom right before boarding. As I anxiously awaited the announcement that we could board, my phone rang. It was Blake.

"Hey, girl."

"Maximo. You're awake, good. I wanted to make sure you didn't miss your flight. You spent the whole day in airports. Oh, Maximo, that sucks. I'm so sorry." She cared about me. I was winning her back.

"Oh yeah, you know it's the small price I have to pay to spend any moment with my favorite girl. We're boarding now. All worth it. I got to spend extra time with you. Blake, do you maybe like me? Even just a little?"

"I'm glad you woke up this time to make your flight." She giggled.

"And?" I asked again sarcastically.

"And Maximo, you're high on my list of people I like."

"Alright, that's good to know. I got to go, but I'll call you to make plans. I'm going to come and see you, my sweet Blake."

"Okay, Maximo. I look forward to it. Be safe, Maximo." Then she hung up the phone. I boarded the plane with a smile and got off in New York with a smile. I ran straight to work even though it was early afternoon. I wanted to use today as turning over a new leaf. I was back to my old self when I was with Blake. My charm was back on, my energy was at a high. Nothing could stop me. After a few weeks of this, my bosses took notice and the red flag on my file went away. It was good. When Blake was in my life, I could do anything. I was everything. I felt alive.

Blake and I spoke every night and sent silly emails during the day. We exchanged sarcasm, oh how I had missed that part. We watched movies together over the phone and had private jokes the next day to the stupid shows we watched the night before. I don't think there was a night during that time that I went to sleep without talking to her. I didn't want to.

I decided to make a surprise trip to Chicago. I knew her plans were going to be quiet for the weekend. I wanted to see her so badly, and from our talks, I thought she would be excited to see me too. I left work and got on the subway straight for LaGuardia. When I got off the plane, I called her to see where the happy hour was. Then I could show up and surprise her there. Her friends would think I was a hero, I'd win them over, and she would see how much I feel for her.

"Hey girl, how is your day going? Are you on your way to happy hour?"

"Hello, Maximo, yes. I'm just leaving the office now. Going to a bar off Wacker. Not sure of the name, but it's on the water. It's a new trendy type of place. Should be fun. How about you?"

"Oh nice, will you be with a bunch of your girlfriends? I'm not sure where I'll be. Perhaps happy hour somewhere. Thinking of you."

"Well, you have a good time then, Maximo. Don't go calling me drunk now!"

"Oh, well then, where is all the fun? Never say never." She laughed and said goodbye.

I grabbed a taxi and headed to a new trendy place off N. Clark and Wacker. I searched through the restaurant and bar, but no Blake. Another, too swanky. Then another. I looked out across the pier to the next restaurant courtyard to find Blake. I walked towards her, still in the other restaurant. She did not see me. Then, when she did, I found she was there with another man. She saw me approaching as I noticed him. She looked up in fear. I guess I didn't know Blake's feelings for me. I guess I didn't know how to feel. I guess I didn't think this moment would ever happen. I guess I didn't know how hard this pain would hurt. I guess I was wrong.

Blake, I thought you loved me, I said in my head, but it was on my face. I turned around in shame and walked as fast as I could to the door.

She called out to me, "Maximo, Maximo!" As she jumped the barrier and ran to grab me. "Maximo, what are you doing here?"

"Don't worry about it," I said and pushed her off me.

CHAPTER TWENTY-FIVE

~

"Maximo! Maximo! Wait, please! Wait." I stopped in my tracks for Blake to run after me as I was doing my best to get to a corner and hail a cab. She grabbed my shoulder. With my height and weight, she was not strong enough to get me to turn myself around. I was fighting back the tears, I was so upset.

"Maximo. I'm so excited that you are here. I really am. I'm so surprised. I wish you would have told me." Blake held her hand on my back as I was panting to hold in tears. I waved again to a cab who signaled that he was stopping for me. As he pulled up, I took the roses I had for her in my hand and tossed them into the trash beside me and went into the cab. I didn't look at her. I caught the rearview mirror watching her stand in the street holding her face in her hands, turning around to see if he followed her as well. There was no one there but Blake on the side of the road alone.

"Where to sir?" The cab driver asked. I had no idea.

"Ugh, I don't know. Take me to a bar. Anywhere. A bar that is happening and where I can meet hot girls and forget the one I just left on that corner.

"Oh, girl troubles, yup. I got a bar for you." He revved up the engine and took a turn. I didn't watch. I was heated and furious. *I am such a fool, such a fool. What was I thinking?*" My head and my heart were bleeding.

I couldn't control my breathing. I need Blake to help me as I was running from her.

The cab pulled up to a bar crowded with young adults drinking and doing their best to forget the week. I would blend right in.

"Thanks, man." I shook his hand and gave him a nice tip. I needed to drown in forgetting Blake. I moved in with my overnight bag to a spot at the bar right behind a brunette nursing her drink. She wanted my attention right away. She was hungry for someone new. She was hungry for someone like me.

"Excuse me, can I just jump in for a quick drink?" I said as I touched her shoulder and moved my finger to dance down her arm as I concentrated on finding a bartender.

"Oh, don't make it quick. Buy me one and stay awhile." I caught the bartender's attention and ordered us a round of drinks and shots as I handed him my credit card. I kept my attention on her. She wasn't that attractive because of her outdated style and hurt on her face. She was washed out from being tired of chasing a man. She wore her badge on her sleeve. We could all see it. She struggled with trying to find a guy tonight. She had been struggling with it for some time. Tonight, I'll make her feel special. Take her back to her apartment, have sex with her. Make her feel special all night long into the morning. Then I will pretend that I will stay in touch and throw out her number in the trash right in front of her building as I hail a cab to the airport where I will sit and wait to get back to New York. I will most likely cry like a fool the whole way. *"Why, Blake, why?"*

Shots, drinks, dancing to stupid music. She was eating up all my mush. I knew what she was looking for. Give the guys she tried to flirt with for years a chance to see her smile. See her in a new light. Maybe want to give her a chance and ask her out next week at happy hour. But not tonight. Tonight, she'll dazzle on the dance floor. Drink too much. Laugh out loud. Feel sexy and wanted. Tonight, they'll notice and wonder who I am. What am I doing here? Why do I think she is so important when they couldn't see it?

We danced and went to sit back at the bar to laugh and share another drink. "So, which one? Which one is it?" I asked her. The men were looking from a table across the room. She giggled and held my hands. I smiled and kept my attention on her. They were watching.

"I don't know what you're talking about," she said and sipped her drink as she weaved from side to side on her stool.

"Which one broke your heart?" She sat back and held her drink intently.

"What? What's this? Are you one of them? Is this some kind of joke?" She clearly had been down this road before. As she was about to get up from the stool and run away, I grabbed her and kissed her.

"No, no. Not at all. I was trying to make you... Ugh, I don't know. These jerks are staring you down, and you're showing off. I was just reading the situation. I'm sorry. I didn't come here to hurt you at all. I'm sorry. I read this wrong. I'll go. Check please!" The bartender brought me over the check, which I signed. I hated to play a mind game on her. I was only here for one night. I needed to mask my hurt and try to make someone else feel better about themselves. Right now, I clearly had not. I was playing a Jedi mind trick on her for my benefit. Lord, please forgive me.

"WAIT, WAIT," she cried. "I'm sorry, I just have been hurt so many times; I'm always on defense. I'm having a blast with you, Max. Is it Max, right? Please stay with me. Have another drink with me. The bar is going to close soon. I don't want to end the night like this. Please. I can't have them watch me and watch you leave. I really can't deal with that right now. Please stay."

I looked out at all the men and their snares and judgment on her. I looked into their eyes, and there it was—her story. I saw it. She wanted attention. She'd been chasing the idea of being in love for so long that she was sad and desperate. She had her heart broken, probably by one of them. Probably more than once, but she came back for more. Each week she sat at this bar waiting for something or someone. But where are they? All of you sit on the other side at a table and whisper about her—how you went out with her and then never called her.

Maybe one of you went out with her hot friend instead—the one who was so nice to look at. She licked her lips when you spoke to her. She wore the lowcut tops that you stared down the entire night. She was in bed, and you did whatever you wanted to her. She just laid there and waited. She was the one who had a low-income job, so you gave her a six-carat ring. She was the one who had your baby, and you built her a white picket fence and a big house. She never lost her baby fat. She ate chips on the couch and waited for you to come home to a house full of crying kids that needed attention. There was no conversation at dinner. No excitement in the bedroom.

But tonight you're here, watching the bridesmaid at your wedding dance with some dashing guy from New York. Why are you here again? Oh, because you don't want to go home tonight and remember the mistake that you made. Tonight, you watched that woman you had intelligent conversation with who knew about politics and sports and had sex with you on her dining room table. Made you excused yourself in a meeting because the thoughts about that night were showing on your face.

Mazzy has a six-figure job and wanted to have your children, but you didn't want that. You wanted a Barbie doll on your arm. She held in her tears and stood in a church where two people she loved betrayed her. You told your wife to stop talking to her. You did the same yourself, for no reason at all. She feels bad about herself like it was her fault. She holds your guilt, but she wasn't good enough for you? Now she's at the same bar as you alone. Suddenly, you're jealous of her. Now you have it. Your Barbie doll wife that you no longer even like is at home with your children. And you are here with your other friends who fall into the same category. All she wanted was to be loved. Her size B chest didn't make the cut. Please, gentlemen, you should be ashamed of yourselves.

I felt horrible as she was hurt far worse than I saw. I know how she felt. I looked at the men at the table and sat back down in the chair.

"Hey, Bartender." I handed the check back to the bartender and whispered into his ear. "Buddy, do me a favor. Buy that table a round of shots and two for us." He nodded and handed out the shots.

"Alright, here's your moment." I turned her around, and we held up our shots to them. We downed it and I grabbed her from the chair, kissed her, and walked her out of the bar. They sat in their sad ties with their watered-down drinks and remembered their moments with her and the regrets they had since the days they hadn't called her back.

We walked to her apartment. I said goodbye as we got to the door-man. "Please, Max, come up with me. Please?" I hate it when people call me Max, but I let it slide.

"What are we going to do upstairs? It's late, and we've had a lot to drink. I don't want to take advantage of you." She looked at the doorman for approval. My body language was serious. I know, I'm playing a game and it's not right. Remember, I miss Blake. Do you see what she does to me?

The doorman nodded that I seemed okay. She led me to the elevator as I saluted the doorman for his approval. Her apartment had an older vibe. She told me her wealthy grandmother left it to her in the will. The antiques and gold painted furniture didn't seem her style. She had books open all around the house. Some about art. Some about business. Some romance novels. She was an avid reader. Her wine glasses were also all over the apartment. It was obvious; she was lonely. Not many people came to visit. There were pictures of her and her family. She was smiling in all their pho-tos. She was a lawyer at a top law firm in Chicago and worked long hours.

The garbage overflowed with take-out containers from all types of cuisine. I'm sure she was on a schedule: Chinese-Monday; Italian-Tuesday; Indian-Wednesday; leftovers-Thursday after happy hour; Friday-happy hour, no dinner; Saturday-bagels, dinner at the diner if not with boring work clients; Sunday-dinner at her parent's house.

I opened a bottle of wine left on the table. I didn't think she skimped on the important stuff. I went to play music; she had mostly classical CDs in her turntable. I dimmed the lights and lit some candles while she was in the bathroom doing some last-minute grooming in a drunken fashion. I could hear her dropping things and cursing under her breath. She needed tonight. I needed tonight. I needed Blake. I couldn't have Blake. I went to check my phone, and there were several messages from Blake and texts that I wasn't going to check at this time. I ignored them all. Tonight, I was with Mazzy.

She came out in a lace number that showed off her assets. Her B cup was very beautiful in what she was wearing. Her clothes did not reveal that at all. Maybe that was part of her problem. She let her hairstyle go, and her make-up was non-existent. The clothes she wore were suits and not fun. She lost all her girlfriends who would help her with these things. I felt like I could become like her if I didn't have Blake. I thought of my mom when my dad decided to stop coming home and how that must have felt like. I felt Mazzy lost in that feeling. She needed this.

I took her by her hand and gave her some wine in the other. We slow danced, and I moved my hands over her body. She was weakening by the touch. It had been too long. I didn't have to put on any moves with her. I didn't even need to sleep with her. I chose not to. Blake would have approved if I cared and all. We danced, and I let her straps fall off her shoulders. I pushed her panties down just slightly enough to get her aroused. She worked diligently to tear my clothes off. I let her know it was okay to go slow. She got me down to my boxers I picked out just for Blake. I couldn't wait for that moment to show them off to her. Now they're tainted by someone else. Mazzy touched my back as we danced and drank wine. We didn't talk. These were just moments of silence. I'm sure she was thinking of someone else. I was thinking of Blake.

We fooled around on her floor in the living room, just as teenagers would in their experimental phase. She laid on my chest as I was sitting up against the couch pulling over a blanket to keep her warm. She fell asleep soundly. I looked out the window and drank wine. *"Blake, where are you? Why must you taunt me so?"* I was in a fog from all the drinks. What was my next move to get to Blake? I didn't know.

Mazzy woke up smiling. Not sure if it was because last night hap-pened. And because I didn't take advantage of her. Or the fact that I was still there. I didn't have the heart to be cruel to her as planned. I also didn't want to be alone in my sadness. I was using her just as she was using me. She didn't know it yet.

"Max. I know this is kind of forward of me. We just met and all. But I have this gallery opening tonight, and I don't have a date. I have an extra ticket, but when I found the guts to ask the guy I really want to go with, it was too late. Now he's going with someone else. I know I'm not your type, but I was hoping that you can be my date? Maybe to make him jealous?"

"Oh, really? So, I do have an answer to the question. There is someone you want to make jealous. Was he there last night?"

"No, he was going to. But his sister came into town and—"

"And, nothing. That's bullshit. No way. Then he disses you for someone else? What is the next excuse on this guy?"

"Well, it's not an excuse, I mean. Well, I don't know. Maybe it is. Forget it. I'm sorry. I feel foolish." She got herself up to run again to the bathroom.

"Mazzy, Mazzy! Wait. Please. I'm happy to accommodate you to the gallery opening. Don't say you are not my type. You don't know who is. I'm here with you now, aren't I? But listen. I'm going back to NY, and the distance thing sucks. So, let's not pretend it will work long term. I want to spend time with you today and tonight. It will be fun. You like this guy anyway, so let me help you win him over. Let me help you be the woman you want to be—the woman I saw last night, laughing and dancing. The one who enjoyed herself. Let me help you find her to find him." She dove in for a kiss. I was thrown back.

"Woo, woo, alright; relax, there's enough of me to go around. Don't wear out the heavy machinery." She laughed at my joke; it was the best way I could tell her the truth in a way that wasn't insulting.

"Oh Blake, why?"

"So, we have some work to do. Go get dressed, let's get out there and get you ready."

CHAPTER TWENTY-SIX

~

I took her to get her hair done into a stylish cut that fit her face. Highlights to give her a little style and a new look. We went shopping for some trendy clothes that she could wear when she goes to happy hour and a sexy dress with heels for tonight. When the day hit early afternoon, we went full of bags and freshly painted nails to a restaurant for a late lunch and a much-needed drink. She was excited; I don't think she gets much girl time or attention from men.

"Max, this day was awesome. I feel like a new woman. I needed this. Thank you ever so much."

I blushed a bit. "I'm glad. So, tell me about this guy you like. Why is he so special?" She took a deep breath and sat back holding her drink looking to the side. She didn't know how to have this type of conversation; she only had it in her head. I felt so bad for her.

"He's not that cute. Kind of a nerd. But to me, he's so handsome. He works in the DA's office. We flirt, or I shamelessly throw myself at him, and he doesn't notice. I don't know what I should do. I ask him to do things, and he sometimes says yes and then has an excuse. I have to say it hurts, but I somehow have this feeling. This voice inside of me keeps telling me to ask again. That he is the one. It sounds so silly saying it out loud."

She looked down in embarrassment, but I understood each word she was saying. It was always how I felt about Blake. Right now, as I told myself that it is over, Mazzy just let me see that it isn't at all. It doesn't have to end here.

"Mazzy, it's not crazy. Not at all. I think you should stick with your gut. Listen to that voice. I feel the same way about someone. I know exactly what you're thinking. It's some sort of sign from above to go and find that person."

"Really? I do believe that! I think we're meant for things in our life to happen. Meet one person to get to the next. Max, I think that I met you to get myself to him. Is that crazy? Are you mad that I'm saying this to you?"

I laughed. She was excited; it was adorable. She was right. We met each other to get to someone else.

"Like six degrees of separation. Maybe, kind of? I believe that. Mazzy, I'm very glad I met you. And now is a good time to tell you something very important."

"Oh yes, Max? What is that?" She was attentive to what I was about to say. I leaned into her and whispered. "Please don't call me Max. It's Maximo." I touched her hand and smiled as I touched her nose with mine and gave her a kiss.

"Oh, yes, Maximo. I'll never call you Max again."

We left in a black car that her firm sent to take us to the gallery event. This was a work affair, and she had her game face on. But I reminded her to have fun. She slipped her arm underneath mine and waited with a dashing, tall, gawky man from New York for the excitement to show up. I was a mystery to everyone, including her. We arrived, flashes in our face from the step and repeat. She stood tall to catch up to my height in the heels she was not comfortable wearing. I bet Blake would be comfortable and confident in them. We walked around, and she giggled when we passed another couple she introduced me to.

"OMG, OMG!" she said under her breath, slapping me. "He's over there, three o'clock! OMG!"

I looked over, and there was the guy—geeky, not in a tux, but in a black jacket and a tuxedo shirt that needed to be ironed, and jeans. He was nervous. He had someone on his arm. I looked to see who it was. An older girl. Aha! It must be his sister. She also was in a plain dress in need of some help. They had the same mannerisms, same hair color, and glasses. They both pushed them back with their middle fingers at the same time. Peas in a pod.

"Mazzy, have you ever thought that maybe he is intimidated by you? Maybe that's why he keeps declining? I mean, you're magnificent, and he's a silly nerd. I mean look at him."

"I'm looking at him. He's adorable, but he's here with someone else. What do I do?" I laughed and turned her around, so he would not notice her.

"Silly Mazzy, that's his sister. Now, this is what we are going to do. We're going to grab some champagne and start heading the other way to conveniently bump into him. Then I'll whisk away his sister to look at some stupid painting a few spaces away and give you some time to talk. If you feel that there's no chemistry, then I'll be close by to get you out of it. If there's chemistry, then politely excuse yourself to me and take him somewhere low key and down to earth. You can do this, girl! Make it happen! I believe in you." I held her arms to have her keep focus. She soaked in every word I said. "Yes, yes!" We grabbed champagne and headed on to our mission.

"Oh hello! I didn't see you." The first encounter was set.

"Hello Mazzy, so nice to see you. I almost didn't recognize you. You're so beautiful tonight."

They stood still, staring into each other's eyes. She had this one in the bag. I took his sister across the way to look at something that had zero meaning to me but gave me some talking points since I had art history down. She rambled on from there. I stood staring at the ceiling and looking among the crowd. I looked back at Mazzy who found her way to loop her arm under his and signal back with a thumb up. I smiled back with my glass of champagne. I came back to the boring conversation that I was not listening to. My mind had wandered elsewhere. My mind was on Blake.

"Maximo, what happened to you. Why are you here?" A whispering voice of concern and a body came up to me holding my arm. It was Blake. I was in shock.

"Why do you care? What are you doing here? Are you with your boyfriend?" I started to walk away from her with my hand in my pocket and the other holding my champagne. I pretended not to be interested in her when all I wanted to do was run away with her forever.

"Maximo, that is so unfair. I didn't know that you were coming. I told you that I couldn't make a commitment. That I'm trying to sort things out."

"So, you are sorting things out with him. Thanks, Blake, it makes sense. I feel better already. Thank you." I continued to walk on.

"Maximo, I like you so much. I'm dating, nothing serious, Maximo. I have to find out who I am. Who the voice is in my head. Who I screamed to when I was laying in the street crushed in a car with my family dead lying in a pool of blood. I'm just trying to find who that person is, Maximo. Please, understand. I—"

I turned around to look at her. The flashes of her laying there, listening to her in my sleep, and calming her down all came back to me. "It was me, Blake. It was me. I was the one who was talking to you the night of your accident. I can tell you what you were wearing, how you were laying down. It all came to me in a dream. I felt like I was there. I had no idea that it was more than a dream, but Blake it was me. When I was at the wedding and found out about your accident, I knew it was real. I care about you so much it hurts. I want to be with you and spend my life with you. Take care of yourself. I don't understand what you're going through, but Blake, I love you and want to learn what it all means. This hurts more than you know."

I walked away again fighting my rage and tears. I found a corner behind the caterer's glasses. I faced the other way and tried to hide my tears.

"Maximo! Maximo! I care about you too. Why didn't you tell me about the dream? Maximo!" I couldn't let her see me cry, but she jumped in front of me. I couldn't hide.

"I couldn't process everything the night at the wedding. I just wanted to spend time with you and not get deep. I don't know, is it real? Because, Blake, I know I was with you that night. I know that was real. It was me who was talking to you, Blake, it was me," I managed to say through my tears.

"Maximo. I don't know if you don't tell me. I want to understand everything. This is so much to handle. I do feel connected to you; I so do. I'm so scared to lose someone again. I have no family and am not sure who I can trust. I don't want to hurt anyone, Maximo. I never want to hurt you. I'm so confused."

She was crying and fell into me for comfort. I couldn't live without her. I hugged her back, and we cried in the dark hallway together. I was starting to let my guard down. I was given another chance to be with my Blake again.

"Maximo? Maximo? Are you back here?" Shit, it was Mazzy. How would I explain this to Blake? I had forgotten I was there with her. I didn't answer, but Blake heard the call and lifted her head up.

"Maximo?" Then Mazzy was right there behind us with her arms crossed. Not because she was upset, just confused. Mazzy was not sure why I walked away to a dark corner with Blake. Neither of them understood the situation.

"Maximo, I, I, I, am..." She was stuttering out of shock. Blake was furious. Pushed me and took off. "Blake, wait! Blake!" I pushed Mazzy away and ran for Blake who even in heels was faster than me. She didn't let me explain. Mazzy was running behind me. Blake jumped into a cab and was pulling away when I got to the door. "BLAKE!" I screamed, and she left me standing on the corner. I looked back to see Mazzy behind me and looked forward to seeing Blake crying in the cab.

"Maximo, I don't know what just happened. How do you know Blake? I was coming to tell you that Zac left with his sister, they had dinner plans with their family. But I'm going to have brunch with him tomorrow. So yeah? I'm sorry, Maximo? What's going on?"

I stood in the street, afraid again that I had made the biggest mistake of my life, and all I wanted to do was to slit my wrists and drown in my blood. Would Blake talk me through it?

Blake, I love you, I love you. Listen to my voice. It's me, Maximo. She's just a friend. Please, Blake, please. Understand it's you. It's always you, my love, I said in my head; I hope she heard me.

"Maximo?" Mazzy said.

I had to get it together. "Yeah, Mazzy, hi."

"Maximo, did I mess something up? Are you with Blake? It looked like you knew each other."

"Yeah, I know her. It's a long story. I'm glad that everything worked out with your man. Any chance we can go?"

"Yeah, of course," she responded. I grabbed our coats. I looked at my phone and listened to the messages from Blake the night before.

"Maximo, where did you go? Please come back, I want to see you."

"Maximo, where are you? Please call me back."

"Maximo, I love you. You are the voice in my head. Maximo, I know it is you. He doesn't mean anything to me. Please Maximo, I only want to be with you."

"Maximo…are you okay?"

It only hurt more and made me look like a jerk. I called her right away.

"Blake, Blake. Please. Mazzy and I just met. She needed me so she could meet someone else. I swear I had no idea you would be here. I just listened to your messages. Please believe me. Blake, I love you so much.

Please. If you don't believe me, you know each other—call her. Please, Blake, please. I love you. I don't want to lose you again. It was me. I heard you. You were signing Journey's "Don't Stop Believing." You wore a white shirt and a checkered blue and white skirt. You had on your red silk underwear and the baby blue gingham bra. That morning you kissed your dog goodbye and grabbed a coffee. I know because I saw you in my dream, Blake. It was me. I love you, Blake; I love you. Please believe me." I was screaming into the phone.

I finally got into the car with Mazzy, and we headed out.

CHAPTER TWENTY-SEVEN

~

We went to a restaurant that we were overdressed for; it was actually perfect to make us laugh and break the ice. We had a drink and then she asked again the question I was not sure how to answer.

"Maximo, are you mad with me?" she asked.

"Mazzy, no. No, not at all. I'm sorry. I know this sounds and looks horrible. But I just got my heart broken."

"By Blake? How do you know her? I answered your question, remember."

"Yes, Mazzy. By Blake. I swear I didn't know she was going to be there. I feel like a jerk. When you told me you knew that you and your man were connected—that's Blake and me. I've been trying to convince her that I am hers forever. But she's having a hard time believing me. Then when you came over, it was confusing to her, and she ran. Ugh. I so messed up."

"So, I'm not sure if you know this. But Blake was in a bad accident and—"

"Yes, I found that out the hard way. She was my love years ago and forgot about me after the accident. I had a dream about it. I swear I was there with her at the accident. We're searching for each other and keep getting intercepted by ridiculousness on both ends. Oh, destiny, you're mean and unfair."

"Wait, wait. Don't be mad at the universe. We met each other for a reason. Blake and I were friends when she lived here when we were very young. My dad and her dad were very good friends through work. I knew her but not that well. She was always so nice. We didn't stay in touch. I saw her once before she went to Switzerland and now that I think of it, she did mention that she was in love. And yes, it was a Maximo. Wow! She doesn't remember me, and well, it's confusing for her. I don't want to upset her, so I say hello when I see her. I'm trying to make a new friendship with her. Do you have a picture of you guys together?"

"I guess we are in each other's life for a reason," I said. "Here, I do have pictures. This is the one I keep in my wallet. She asked not to see any pictures because she wants to learn about our energy. I can scan them and send them over to you when I get home."

"Yes! I've seen this! She has it too. Yes, I heard about her not wanting to look at pictures. Let's make a game plan, Maximo. We have to get you back to her!"

Mazzy was so full of enthusiasm, my belief in my relationship with Blake came back. I was not giving up on getting her back. I gave Mazzy a big hug. I felt better already.

"Maximo, I owe you so much. This weekend changed my life. I would be honored to get you and Blake back together. I'm grateful that you gave me the confidence to get me to the man I lusted over for years. We're connected. I believe in that."

"I do too; I'm so glad. You're a guardian angel to me too."

We went back to her place, and I insisted that I sleep on the couch.

"Maximo, I know this is crazy. We just met and had an intimate night together. You were such a gentleman and didn't press me for anything. It was so lovely. I'm embarrassed to ask this, but can you stay with me in my bed? I haven't been with a man in years; you were so warm and comforting. I want to have another night with you. We don't have to do anything. Just sleep. It just feels so good to have someone to sleep next to you. I don't want anything more," Mazzy said timidly, embarrassed by the request.

"Come here," I signaled her to come over, and I brought her into a hug. I needed someone too. We drank some wine and talked about her date with Zac tomorrow. She was nervous, and I reassured her. I told her not to act like the man but to let him lead even though she had been taken advantage of through the years. It's sad how you fall into a pattern and let people take advantage of you. I wanted her to have happiness, find love. She deserved to be loved. She was a wonderful person; so many men had tried to ruin that for her.

We went to sleep, and I let Mazzy cuddle with me. I was glad because I needed someone too.

"Blake, Blake. I miss you so much. Let me please explain. I only want to be with you, Blake. Give me a chance, Blake." I said in my head and hoped that it would be enough to get to her.

I woke up at four. Blake woke up every morning at four am to use the bathroom, get a drink of water, and then go back to bed. She didn't sleep much after that. She used that time to collect her thoughts. I woke up every day at four am to feel Blake get up, even if we are in different places. I just always felt connected to her.

Following her routine this morning, I woke up and left the bed. I went to the kitchen where Mazzy couldn't hear me and at four am I gave Blake a call. She answered.

"Maximo."

"Blake, thank you for answering. Did you get my messages?"

"Maximo, I didn't listen to them. Who were you there with? Why are you with someone else?"

"Blake, I want to be with you. I always only want to be with you. I was genuine with what I told you. I did dream of you the night of your accident. I was the one talking to you. You are questioning me about a friendship that I have. Who is the guy you were with? Is he telling you stories of how in love you were once upon a time? That you wake up every day religiously at four am? That you love red Twizzlers when you watch a movie? How you belch after drinking a beer? How you make me so happy? Blake, please can we meet up and talk? Please?"

"Well, no. No one is telling me these things. No one but you. Maximo, I like you so much. I'm scared."

"Blake, meet me. I can come to you. I want to see you. I know you're scared. I'm scared too. I'm scared that you're going to continue to run away from me, and I'm going to lose the love of my life. Blake, I want to spend my life with you. Have children with you. Be your husband. Let me prove to you that I'm the one, Blake. I don't want to lose another minute with you." The phone was silent. I could still hear her on the other end. "Blake?" I asked, to make sure.

"Maximo, meet me at Elaine's Coffee Call. It opens at six-thirty."

"Yes, Blake, see you then." I fumbled around to get dressed and left Mazzy a note. I headed out with no time to think about seeing Blake again.

I arrived at the coffee shop. She was already there with a cup of coffee. She was for sure torn about what she wanted. I could see it in her face. I went in and flew into the chair across from her in a way to make her laugh and hopefully to lighten the mood. I grabbed her hands. She had tears in her eyes.

"Blake. I want to take away your pain. We had something special. I know you don't remember that. I don't want to harm you. I can tell you're torn on who to trust. So, what is it that I can do to get you to that point? Did you not see any pictures of us? Do you still wear my flannel to bed? The green and white one? My hat from high school? You wore it all the time. Blake, I know you want to move forward, and I want to move forward. I want to move forward with you.

"Mazzy was someone I met when I left you Friday night. She's a very nice wonderful person. She told me her dad used to have a working relationship with your dad when you were young. She knows who you are. I'm sure you don't remember that. She didn't know anything about you and me. I didn't know about her either. I set her up with a man she was in love with for years. She's going on a date with him today. I'm just her friend. We realized that right away. But you're with someone? I'm not doing anything wrong here, Blake. I just wanted to surprise you. We talk every night. I can't sleep without you."

"I know Mazzy. She's a very high-profile lawyer. I noticed her change at the gallery. I noticed her with you, and I was very jealous. I was jealous because I like you, Maximo. I didn't understand it until then. But I do have feelings for you. I've been dating the guy I was with for a few weeks. He's nice, but—"

"But? There shouldn't be a but, Blake."

"But, he's not you. I want to be with you." I held her hands tighter and closed my eyes.

"Then Blake. Let's make plans to make that happen. Let's not wait any longer."

She looked to the side and back at me. "I haven't been seeing him that long. Yes, I'll let him go. I have to do one thing, Maximo. I need to look into one thing. I found someone on LinkedIn. His name is Ben, an investment banker. I remember him from middle school. I haven't remembered anyone. I haven't told anybody because I want to see him and know for sure. I have such feelings for you, Maximo, but I don't want to wonder forever what if? If we're real, then we're real. It'll just be a foolish exercise. I'm forever confused, and I want to look at this last avenue. If you love me, Maximo, then you'll understand."

I closed my eyes again and brought my head down to the table. I could not believe this. "Blake, I do love you. Let me take care of you. If this is the way to prove to you that I'm the one, then go and find him. But, please understand, I'm genuine. Talk to Mazzy, let her tell you that I'm for real."

"Maximo, I'll reach out to him and meet up with him, so I'll know. I want to know."

"Alright, Blake. Alright. I get it. You're still stubborn. You're still irresistible. Blake, I'll wait until you can be mine. It'll hurt the whole time."

"Thank you, Maximo. I know in my heart what I want to do. Thank you for letting me do this."

"So, what is it that your heart is telling you to do?" I asked with a smirk, hoping that this would be the way she would tell me I was the one.

"I'll let you know when you need to know," she said with a smile. Her eyes looked into mine. She released her anxiety, sat back, and let go of my hands as she took a sip of her coffee. She was comfortable with me again.

"Oh, Blake, I love the games you play. Don't go falling in love with someone else now. Or else."

"Or else what?" She leaned back in as close as she could.

"Or I'm going to have to scold you. Now, you wouldn't like that. Or would you?"

"I guess you'll have to wait and see."

I leaned in for a kiss. "Blake, you drive me over the moon crazy. Don't make me wait forever."

"I won't."

We finished our coffee and said a long goodbye through passionate kisses. I left her and headed back to Mazzy and crawled back into bed with her. She awoke.

"Maximo are you okay?"

"Yes, Mazzy, go back to sleep. I pulled her in to snuggle again. I went to sleep with a smile on.

"Blake, I'm serious. Don't fall for someone else."

As I fell asleep, I saw her running through a field, turning around to send me a kiss. She heard me.

When we woke up for the day, Mazzy leaned on her side and touched my chest.

"Maximo. Tell me what to do to please Zac? I mean, in bed. What do guys like?" I looked at her with a smile. She really was so smart and so naïve at the same time.

"You're thinking too much. Don't overthink it. Do what comes naturally. Ask him what he wants. Make sure you look at him in the eye and smile. Be kind. Don't act like a dirty slut because that's what your girlfriends told you to do. Just be you, Mazzy. He likes you; I know it."

She was embarrassed and didn't want to mess it up. Her face was red. She was fantasizing bringing him back here and repeating what we did a few nights ago and taking it the step forward she had forgotten about. She was burning for it.

"Maximo, I'm serious. You're an angel. How are you so great? How does Blake not see that?" I took hold of the strands of hair on her forehand to push them back off her eyes.

"You are kind, Mazzy. I know that Blake is confused. I want to do the right thing and make her my wife. I know in my heart that she's mine. I have to wait. This waiting stuff sucks." I got up to get dressed and went out to help her clean up her kitchen of the takeout containers that were all over the place. She needed to tidy up if she were going to have real company. I was happy with how the weekend turned out. Maybe not getting what you want when you want it makes you fight harder to get it. Makes you see who you really are. I'm happy that I met Mazzy. She let me see my situation in a new way. God is watching over me. I know it will work out.

"Did you just clean up in here?" Mazzy asked when she came out of the bedroom.

"Yes, Mazzy. Please keep this place clean. No guy wants to come to a messy house. But don't make it too perfect, just not gross messy." I kissed her on her forehead. "Thank you for the hospitality, my dear, along with a new friendship I'm grateful for. Now do good on this date and let me know how it goes." I grabbed my bag and headed out.

"Maximo, you're the best. I don't know how to thank you."

I just smiled and waved as I closed the door and headed to the airport.

CHAPTER TWENTY-EIGHT

~

Mazzy went on her brunch date with Zac. She pushed her nerves away and wore an outfit I picked out for her with heels. I told her she should practice wearing heels as often as possible. Zac met her at the front of the restaurant and brought a bouquet of colorful Gerber daisies for her, which happened to be her favorite. He wore a tee shirt and a dinner jacket with jeans. She wore a very trendy dress with her hair down in curls. Right away he went to touch one as he came in for a hug. She blushed.

They ordered Bloody Mary's—one spicy and one not. She had the Eggs Benedict; he had an omelet. They spoke about work topics that turned into the art gallery showing and what pieces they liked best. Her nerves faded after the second Bloody Mary that eventually turned into a chilly walk along the lake. He held her hand, and she made sure she smiled. He asked her to see a show on Wednesday night, which turned into late night drinks. Dinner on Friday and a sleepover come Saturday. Sunday brunch all over again. She felt like a woman; he was kind to her and made her feel like a queen each time they came together. After a few weeks, he moved into her apartment. That Christmas he gave her a ring and promised that he wanted to spend the rest of his life with her. She wanted nothing more.

"Maximo! I want you to be the first to know! I got engaged! I can't believe it. I got engaged!"

"Mazzy, that's awesome. I'm so happy for you. See, I knew all along what you needed."

"Maximo, I for sure owe you everything. You seriously helped me make this happen. You HAVE to come to the wedding!"

"I will, for sure. It would be my honor."

"Thank you, Maximo! How are you btw? Still talking to Blake?"

"Uh, well we talk, not a lot. But it's okay. She needs to find herself. I promised I would give her space."

"Yeah, but Maximo. That was like months ago. How long does she need?"

"I don't know. I don't know what to do."

"Maximo, do what you told me to do—follow my heart and be myself. Why are you questioning it?"

"You know what? You're right. I am overthinking it. Thank you, Mazzy. Once again you have given me hope."

"Go for it, Maximo! I know you love her. So don't hold back!"

We hung up the phone. I thought of nothing more than Blake. I wanted to reach out to her every day. I wanted to be with her. Why am I holding back? Did she really see this guy? Am I allowed to ask her? It was Christmas. I needed to have some resolution on this. I gave her a call.

"Hey, Maximo, Merry Christmas. How are you?"

"Hey, girl. How are you? Merry Christmas. Thinking of you. Wanted to say hi."

"Hi, Maximo, I miss you too."

"So, we haven't really talked much about us. I wanted to give you the space you needed. But it's Christmas, and I do want to see you again because I still feel the same for you, Blake. I mean it. I want to be with you." The silence came over us again.

"Maximo. I know you do. You've been kind to not pressure me. I enjoy every conversation that we have. I did reach out to that guy I remembered. I've seen him."

"And?"

"Well, he was sweet. I remember so minimal about him, but I do remember him. He's married and has a few kids. But Maximo, I also have feelings for him and have been dating him. I know that it's wrong. I know that it is. He said he's going to leave his wife for me. I'm scared. I don't know if I feel that way about him or have those feelings for you. I'm more confused than before."

"Blake, seriously? Seriously? Blake. I love you. I can't help that you don't remember me. Is that really what's important? I want to marry you and start a family with you! I told you I wanted to give you space to figure this out, Blake. But come on. Him? Really? Do you see yourself marrying this guy and raising his kids? Damn you, Blake. I see our kids. I see us together. I want to be with you, Blake."

"Maximo. I don't know. I see myself with you also, I just—"

"Come on, Blake, come on. Then be with me. BE WITH ME! Let's get together. I'm in Miami. Come here and meet my mom. Be with us. Be with me. Go and find the pictures of us. The clothes of mine that you have. Go find them and see how good we were together. Blake, I want to make you so happy. Just let me. Give me a chance. I'll give you anything you want, Blake. I want to spend my life with you. This guy, so why hasn't he left his wife yet? Is he even going to do it? Is that who you want to be?"

"Maximo, I know it sounds horrible. But I do also have a connection with him. I have a connection with you. Maximo, I need to figure this out."

"Blake, how long? It's been forever. I'm having a hard time holding on and watching you continue to be with other guys. When am I going to be enough for you?"

"Maximo, that's not fair."

"Blake, you're the one not being fair. You want to be with me and then ask for a break to find someone else. It's been killing me and to find out that you are with someone else instead of me crushes me. I can't take this anymore, Blake. I just can't." I hung up the phone and threw it onto the bed.

It was Christmas day, and I was crushed. This was my mom's favorite holiday. She always made it a big deal. We went out to Mass that day and came home to Mom cooking up a storm for her friends who would come by later on.

She was in a good place; I liked her when she was like this. Her life here was easy. She had a great job and a nice condo that looked out over the ocean. She had great friends. She was back to dancing and singing as she cooked. It reminded me of when I was a kid. So, in my head, I went all the way back to that place and put Blake under the rug for now. Today was Christmas, and I had my mom all to myself.

We poured wine and sang the holiday music as I helped her chop garlic and followed her directions to make the dishes she loved the most. I wanted to learn how to cook and to someday have a wife that I could dance with in the kitchen and make fabulous dishes together. Who was I kidding? I only wanted it to be Blake.

The doorbell rang, and the door opened. No one waited for proper invitations to enter. Down here everyone was family. They didn't put barriers between them. A group of men and women entered cheering and kissing each other in praise of this Christmas day. I instantly was in love with their energy.

They came in and took over the party. Someone opened more wine. Someone opened cabinets and brought out glasses. Someone was in the fridge putting a dish together and then shuffled everyone to the deck. My mom's dishes had fingers tasting and adding spices and sharing the spoon to taste. Each person had an opinion and a contribution. Our time together was now a party. I understood why my mom wanted to be here.

The drinks flowed; the dinner was amazing. Each one of them told crazy stories of trips they went on and the parties they attended in Miami. They each shared how they planned the new year and just how the moment was so joyful. They praised in gratitude often and just made me feel like I was part of their family. The party went into the late evening; it never stopped. I was enjoying the feeling. If I wasn't with Blake, this was the best distraction. I loved my mom being happy. I loved her new life.

CHAPTER TWENTY-NINE

~

I went back to New York and yet desperately wanted to return to Miami. It was calling me. I spoke to my mom about how she felt about me invading her world. She was ecstatic. Our connection came back. Blake was kept in that special place that I tried not to touch. I still thought about her. I still wanted her. I am giving her space. I roamed the streets of New York on New Year's Eve and thought hard of what I wanted to do with my life. I was dwelling on Blake, and it was killing me. I needed new space. I needed to move on. I listened to the words that my mom said to me. "If it is meant to be, then God will find a way." If I was meant to be with Blake, I had to let her go and find her way back to me. For now, I need to experience life and live it. I want to live my life.

I found a great job at a software start-up selling to banks in Miami. I was going to be able to have a nice executive job and a very fun lifestyle. I went back to becoming the entertainer and gaining new clients. In Miami, it was an adventure. I moved into the same building as my mom, which felt great. It was like a college dorm. She had her privacy; I had mine. I wasn't clear if she were dating some of the men that I met, or if they were just friends. She was happy and enjoying herself. I met women; they never wanted to make a commitment. I wanted to be free. It was perfect for me. But then there was Ramona. She was a friend of my mom's and closer to my age than the rest of my mom's friends. She was fascinating—so self-confident and unapologetic. She was originally from Cuba, moved here when she was younger, and knew this town inside and out. She knew everyone and when she walked into a room, everyone paid attention. I was mesmerized by her—her long straight black hair, piercing blue eyes, and golden skin. It was almost unreal. Her curves were perfect. She was a boss and let everyone know it. I needed the distraction of Ramona if I couldn't have Blake. I sat back and watched when she came to visit my mom. She came by to ask my mom for advice on silly things while I knew she already had the answers. It was a game she played to draw people to her. She gave me the cold shoulder on purpose. I caught her looking at me from time to time. She was an interesting challenge. Her hair whipped around as she walked, and she was obnoxious about it. Everything about her was obnoxious. She came in like a hurricane and left as a category storm. She was her own show.

I was intrigued by her and let her childhood game of ignoring me play itself out. I met up with my mom and some friends after work one night, and of course I knew that Ramona was going to be there. I put on my best to play her game. I didn't pay attention to her hurricane entrance. I flirted with other girls. I talked with my mom and some of her boyfriends. Having this relationship with her was great. I caught Ramona checking me out and following behind me. When I went to the bar, she stood beside me.

"Maximo, buy me a drink." She didn't hesitate to believe I wouldn't. This was part of her game. Men fell for it. I made her work for it.

"Me? No, you're good. I think that guy over there wants to buy you a drink." I pointed across the bar, signaled to the bartender for mine, and went on my way. She chased me.

"Why won't you buy me a drink, Maximo?" Ramona asked, doing her best to intimidate me in front of my mom and her boyfriend. I turned around to face her along with the crowd.

"Oh Ramona, I'm not one of your toys. Now go along and find someone to play with." I turned back. My confidence was on point, and she didn't know how to break me. She stood there a bit embarrassed and brushed it off, flinging her hair in my face to get a reaction. I continued to sip my drink.

"Nice move, Maximo, I brought my boy up to be a strong and sexy confident man. I like this Maximo in Miami."

My mom gave me a shove and then pulled me in for a hug. We sat at a table and enjoyed our drinks together. As the night came to an end for me, I caught Ramona waiting for me to leave. She followed me to the door, slipping behind me.

As I got out, I said to her, "Can I help you?"

"Maximo, let's take a cab together and go somewhere intimate." She touched my back and looked at me intensely. I didn't budge.

"No, I'm good, Ramona. I'm going home. Big day tomorrow." My cab pulled up, and I got in. She didn't even know I hit her back with her own medicine.

My phone rang an hour later. "Hello?"

"Maximo, let me come over. I want to have another drink. The night doesn't have to be over," Ramona pleaded.

"For me, the night is over," I said. I was already almost asleep, and she was drunk. She didn't know how to be turned down.

"Maximo, I have an event I'm running at the club Friday night. Be my date?"

"Maybe."

"Maybe? Anyone in Miami would love to be my date, and I asked you. Why do you resist me so?" she asked. Her drunkenness gave her confidence.

"I'll check my calendar. Good night, Ramona." I hung up the phone.

She left a text a half hour later with the address and where to pick up my ticket. I was sad that she was so desperate for my attention. But I was desperate to be distracted. I went into my closet where I had a box of pictures and a few things of Blake's. I could not throw them away. I sat in the closet and went through them. My favorite was of Blake and me at her shore house, sitting on the deck after a long night of making love. We were relaxed. I loved how she curled into me—the look in her eye and the danger in her lips. I remembered that night and played it out again in my head. What I would do to go back to that place!

My Blake, I love you so. Don't give up on us. Follow your heart, my love. Follow the love that Jesus gave you to bring you back to me. I want to make you so happy, Blake. Come back to me. I won't disappoint you."

I hope that she heard me.

CHAPTER THIRTY

~

I went to the event on Friday night to see what Ramona had in her. I walked around the crowded club filled with twenty-somethings, too young for my taste. I made my way to the bar to order a drink and was going to walk around and look for Ramona.

"He's with me." The voice came from behind me. My drink was handed to me with a nod, and I turned around to see Ramona.

"Why, hello Ramona, nice party."

"Thank you for coming, Maximo. I hope that you'll enjoy yourself." She nodded and signaled me to the dance floor. It was too early for me to start dancing. My clubbing days were over. I wasn't drunk enough and felt very old in this party.

"Yeah, Ramona, I'm not much of a dancer. I don't know." She turned her shoulders back and forth in front of me and grabbed my empty hand to spin her around. She looked me in the eyes and wanted to seduce me. It was a bit uncomfortable. Her tactics were old. For someone so pretty I could see the desperation in her. I hoped mine didn't show as loud as hers did. I smiled and did my best to move my legs and spin without showing how silly it all looked.

The drinks kept coming and coming. I loosened up; Ramona kept the seduction going. I just played along. I was watching her, but it was just a confirmation for me that I wanted to be with Blake. My mind drifted to picture her sitting at a table in a restaurant with a man who was going to leave his wife. Maybe she was losing faith in it. Perhaps her mind was drifting off to picture where I am. I hope she can't see me here. I don't want to be doing this.

Oh, Blake, I don't want to be with her. I want to be with you, Blake. It's always you.

My mood changed to somber, and Ramona noticed as she grabbed my face to bring my attention back to her. I turned my head because I didn't have a choice. She could see in my face that I wasn't that interested in her. I could see the desperation that she wanted to make me hers and that perhaps someday I could be convinced to love her and take her out of this world of parties that never ended. The crowd that got younger and younger must have reminded her that she was getting older and older. It was a lonely place to be. She didn't want to have to find someone else again. She was tired. I was alone. She came in for a kiss, and I let her. I pulled away after the lingering peck and smiled as she held me in close.

"Are you ready to get out of here?" she asked, and I nodded yes. She took me to her apartment that was on the other side of town. It was very eclectic, filled with lots of scarves on the walls, candles, low to the ground furniture, and big pillows. It was dark and not my style. She burned incense after we entered and led me to the deck with another cocktail. She lit a joint and asked me to share it with her. I didn't want to go back into that world, so I declined. I really declined because I felt that Blake would not approve. She still felt that my energy was not into her, but she didn't give up. Ramona took her clothes off and sat back in her skimpy bra and G-string that became just a G-string when I didn't react. She was hoping that I was going to take advantage of her. She laid back in her lounge chair with her arms above her head as if she were hoping for a tan from the moon. All I wanted to do was to go home. She anxiously awaited me. I finished my drink and politely excused myself for the evening.

"Maximo, wait. Don't go. Come back on the porch with me. Don't you love the night air? It's so refreshing. Enjoy it with me. Keep me warm."

"I think you can put on a sweater. Listen, tonight was great. I don't want to lead you on. I'm not interested in a relationship right now." She pulled me toward her wanting to kiss me, but thankfully I'm so tall she could not reach in her bare feet.

"Oh, Maximo. I know all the women out here say they don't want a relationship to get to you. Men say it too. I believe you do want a relationship. I can see it in your eyes. Now stop being so darn cute and let me take care of you." She was unbuttoning my shirt and moving down to my pants. I pulled away.

"Ramona, I am honest. I don't want to hurt you. I do want to be in a relationship. I have someone else in my heart. She's very special to me. I'm sorry, I don't want to hurt you. Please, understand." I walked away and got closer to the door this time.

"Maximo. I know it's not me. But please, I've been throwing myself at you for months. I want one night with you. Don't make me beg for it." Her desperation was now in the open. I stood at the door contemplating what to do. I don't have Blake. I don't want to be alone either. It was just going to be for one night. One night, right? Oh, I don't want to do this.

Ramona came behind me kissing my back and reaching forward to undo my buttons again. I gave in. We had meaningless sex on her living room floor and ended back on the lounge chairs as the sun came up. I left her sleeping and quietly left her apartment.

I went straight to see my mom before I went to my apartment and felt shameful. She cooked me breakfast, and we talked as we sipped a second cup of coffee.

"Maximo don't beat yourself up. She knew what she was getting into. She's much older than you. MUCH older than you. She's been desperate for years. Her game is old, and she doesn't know how to change it up. She thinks that finding someone young will keep her young. She needs a grown-up job and to date grown-ups. She knew what she was going to lose. Let it be her sadness, not yours. There's always someone else. I know you hide from me that you still like Blake. It's written on your face. She'll come around, I believe it, Maximo. I do." My mom was my best friend.

When we were in sync, everything was good. I went to my mom for a comforting hug. She made me feel like it would be alright.

CHAPTER THIRTY-ONE

~

It was another gallery opening in Chicago, and Mazzy was so excited that it was close to her wedding day. This event was a chance to show off her ring to the friends she lost because she didn't fit into their married circles. As much as she thought this was her ticket to rejoin them, she also felt it was a chance to find new friends that appreciated her for who she was and not what she wasn't. They were a bit washed out. Now Mazzy was in a place where she shined. It felt good.

Her and her fiancé Ben walked through the gallery, enjoying the art and discussing if they should purchase a piece for their new place and where it could fit perfectly. Mazzy turned her head and saw Blake. They hadn't run into each other in a few months. Blake didn't remember Mazzy from childhood, but Mazzy remembered her. Mazzy was so determined to help me get Blake back and was upset to see her there with another man. She followed Blake into the bathroom, creating an encounter together. She was waiting in the sitting area for Blake to leave.

"Hi, Blake," Mazzy said as she stood up to shake her hand and block the exit.

"Hi, Mazzy, right?"

"Yes, I wasn't sure if you would remember me or not."

"Yes, I know you from social circles and the last few gallery openings. I also believe you're a friend of Maximo."

"Yes. I am a friend of Maximo. He's a wonderful person. He helped me find my fiancé. Blake, I know that you don't remember me and that's fine. But I need to give you this. Mazzy opened her purse and handed Blake a picture from long ago that I gave her of Blake and me. She stood back, not sure if she overstepped her boundaries or not. Blake looked at the picture and looked back up at Mazzy.

"What is this? When was this? Who is that? That's me? With who?"

"Yes, Blake. Maximo gave it to me. I've been carrying it around, hoping to run into you. Blake, I don't want to overstep here. Maximo loves you. So much. You were so in love with him back then. Before you left for Switzerland, you told me about him and held the same photo in your wallet. He's such an amazingly genuine person. Blake, I want you to know that. His love for you is for real." Blake sat on the couch and held the photo to her chest. She remembered something.

"Thank you, Mazzy, but I'm engaged to someone else."

"What? No! NO! You can't be. Please, give Maximo a chance. I don't know this guy, but I know about him. He runs a shady business and is mean to his employees. He cheated on his wife the whole time they were married. Are they still married? Oh, please Blake, don't say he's the one. He just can't be!" Blake looked at the photo again. She felt something.

"Thank you for this Mazzy. But I have to go." She ran out of the bathroom and left the gallery with her fiancé at her side. She felt something. She remembered something. She remembered me.

That night she went into her closet after her fiancé fell asleep and found the box that had items from before the accident. She knew one day she would be strong enough to go through them. Today was that day. She opened the box to find my flannel—the green and white one I told her about—and then the hat. She put them both on and smelled them. Her feelings came back to her. She remembered first meeting me in the kitchen and then dancing with me alone at night. . .the passionate kisses we shared. . .the parties we took over. . . making love in her bedroom and how gentle I was with her in the morning. She remembered and cried. She wanted them back.

"Maximo, it is you. I know now that it is you. I made a mistake, Maximo. I remember you," she said and hoped that I heard her.

Blake cried in her closet with the memories she thought would never return. It was heartbreaking to go through all these years, fighting her feelings, looking for something else. She was with someone else. Suddenly she didn't even understand why. Blake grabbed her laptop and went back into the closet. She looked up Mazzy on LinkedIn and connected with her right away.

She emailed Mazzy: Thank you for the picture. I want to meet with you. I want to talk to you about what you know about my fiancé. Is what you said true? I also want to talk about Maximo. Please don't tell him yet that I have the picture. Let me know when you're free. Here's my number. Thank you, Mazzy. —*Blake*

Blake crawled back into bed with the fiancé. She now saw him in an entirely different light. She closed her eyes and saw herself running in a field and signaling me to come. I was chasing after her.

"Blake, I will always be chasing after you. Always."

The text message came through at six forty-five am.

"Hi Blake, it's Mazzy. I can clear my schedule today for whatever time you want to meet up."

Blake ran into the bathroom to text back.

"Thank you, Mazzy. Can you meet me at eight am? Starbucks on N. Clark Street?

"See you then."

Both women met up on a secret mission to find me. Mazzy followed through on her promise. I knew that Blake would be back in my heart in no time.

"Mazzy. Thank you for giving me the picture of Maximo. I remember him. I do. I can't believe it. I found the pictures that I had boxed away. I never went into that box since the accident. I felt the memories. I am so foolish not have looked at them sooner to remember him. I do love him; I know it is him."

"Blake! I'm so excited. I'm so excited, oh my gosh, this is amazing! He'll be so happy to see you and hear this from you."

"Mazzy, wait. I still have to deal with Ben. You said something that triggered me to think about some of his past actions. We're engaged, but he isn't 100% divorced from his ex-wife. It makes me wonder. He's so helpful and interested in my family businesses and wants to help me out. I'm starting to think all of this is not genuine. I was starting not to trust him. So, do you think it's true?"

"Blake, I'm a lawyer in this town. I can't reveal confidential information, but I can tell you that your intuition is probably true. Did you sign any contracts with him? What does he know about your family businesses? What does he want to do?"

"My dad owned a lot of real estate and has an import/export business along with some investments in start-ups and buy-outs. I think Maximo told me that your dad used to be a business partner? Anyway, he has a business investment and wants me to sell off some of the real estate and invest it into crypto coin. It all sounds weird to me. I had him pitch it to my team, and they haven't signed off yet. But they also don't want to hurt my feelings so instead of saying no, they'll procrastinate. He's becoming cold and has an arrogance towards me that I don't like. It's becoming a turn-off. I don't know what I saw in the memory of him from before. I remembered kissing him in middle school. But now, it seems like it wasn't a good memory."

"You did kiss Ben in middle school. Then he told everyone that you gave him oral sex, which I know was not true. I know because I was in the bathroom when you came in crying and told me what happened. He was forcing you to do something you didn't want to. He really embarrassed you, and the guys all believed him. He was nasty in spouting off the made-up details. He's a jerk. He's playing you. Don't sign anything. I honestly would not trust him. I can help you. Let my team investigate further. It would be my honor."

"Did I go to school with you?"

"Yes, we did. We weren't all that close, but you were always nice to me. We talked because of our fathers, and that is when you told me about Maximo. You had already moved to New York, and I always stayed in Chicago. You were so in love with him. All you were doing was showing him off. I could tell in your face how much you felt for him."

"Wow, Mazzy. I don't remember. I'm sorry. But I'll take you up on the investigation. Help me get to Maximo. What should I do?"

"Great. I can come by your office with a colleague this afternoon. BTW, my dad is still an associate with your businesses. So, I hope that makes you feel better. Well, I met Maximo because he came to surprise you. You were with someone else, and he went to a different bar and found me. He made me feel so special. He was such a gentleman to me, didn't try anything, and was just polite and so sweet. He told me that there was someone else. We talked, and he helped me change my look and get to Zac. I owe him everything. We stayed friends; I promised I would help him get back to you. He's always trying to get back to you."

"Where can I find him? I'll show up in Miami and try to get him back. Oh my gosh, is that crazy?"

"Nope, it's love."

CHAPTER THIRTY-TWO

~

I did my best to disengage myself from Ramona. She came by my office with coffee some afternoons. She flirted her way through the office, and I'd come back from a meeting to find her sitting on my desk. Ramona told everyone I was her boyfriend. I wasn't. I didn't do anything past that night with her and made it clear that I was not interested. She said she was fine with it, but she wasn't. It became hard to manage. My boss questioned what she was about. She snooped around my desk. Sometimes I caught her in the lobby of my apartment building, saying she was seeing a friend. From time to time she was seeing my mom. She was using her to get to me. I had a stalker in Miami.

I met my mom for dinner on Thursdays. We had our set spot, and it was my chance to take my mom out on a date and not have to worry about seeing a sleazy girl. It is fun to be flirted with and kiss a sexy woman, but it became cheap, and I didn't want any of it. I laid low and hung out with my mom when she wasn't on a date with someone else. I enjoyed our time together as friends. She was fun and full of life. I understand how my dad loved her when he did. I don't understand why they're not together anymore and how he jumps from woman to woman. Maybe he does what I was doing when I needed to disappear from missing Blake. I so miss Blake. I was running from woman to woman. I'm done with that. I don't want to be with someone else. I only want my Blake.

We finished our dinner, and Ramona showed up just as we ordered the check. She sat herself down and ordered herself a glass of wine, asking the waiter to put it on our check. She didn't ask us if it was okay. I shook my head. She was disgusting. I didn't like her. My mom was done with her coming around. She was a user and not a nice person. We sat there in silence as her wine came and the check, I signed it and finished my drink, asking my mom if she was ready to leave.

"Oh, you're not going to stay with me as I finish my wine?" Ramona asked loudly to try to intimidate us to stay. My mom didn't want to make a scene but followed my lead. We stood up. I fixed my jacket and held in my cool before I responded.

"No, I have to go. Early morning tomorrow at work." Ramona stood up and fell into me, spilling wine on my jacket. It was such a scene. I brushed it off and took my mom out of there. We went somewhere else for a drink and to cool off from being with Ramona.

"Mom, I know she's your friend. She sucks. I seriously regret anything I did with her. She won't leave me alone and stalks me. It's creepy. When do I call the cops? She comes to my job. I can't deal with her. It makes me sick. I don't know what to do other than to be nasty to her. I hate to be like that. I really do." I was clearly upset by this situation, and my mom was there for me. I needed her right now.

"Maximo, I didn't know she was so horrible. I'm so sorry that she's acting like this. Tell the people at your job that she's not allowed to visit you anymore. Tell the building guards that she's not allowed in anymore. I hope that will give her a hint. Ghost her away."

"That's hard here. It's a small place."

"She manipulates people. I think people are sick of her games. I'm sick of her games. Do what you can, and we'll deal with the rest when we get to that. I love you, Maximo. I don't want anyone to hurt my baby."

"Thanks, Mom." While we walked home, I held my mom on my arm as if she were my date for the evening. When we arrived at the building,

I went to the front desk to ask them to no longer allow Ramona to be our guest to the building.

"Sir, she's here now. I think she went up about an hour ago. She had keys and went straight up; I have a signature that is yours, allowing her up. I don't know when you signed it. There's also another guest here for you; she just got here. A blonde lady, very elegant if I may say. Let me look her up. A Blake? When I called up, Ramona said to let her up."

"Wait, what? I never signed anything. Can I see that?" He showed me the signature book. "I never gave her permission. She forged my signature. She's in my apartment now? Blake is too?"

I ran to the elevators up to the twenty-second floor and ran into my apartment screaming for Blake. I walked in to see Ramona in her underwear on my couch and Blake standing there with a bag packed. Ramona was drinking my best scotch.

"So, you came to see my boyfriend Maximo? Packed bag and all? Oh dearest, what did you expect to find here? Maximo is not interested in you; he has me." Ramona said as she stood up to walk towards me running through the door screaming out for Blake.

"No, no you are not my girlfriend! You bitch, how did you get into my apartment?" She dangled my keys in front of me.

"You gave me a set, dearest."

"No, I didn't!" I checked my pockets only to see that my keys were missing. She must have stolen them when she spilled the wine.

"Blake, she is lying. I am not with her; she stole my keys! Look I have wine all over me. She fell into me as she crashed dinner with my mom. She must have stolen them then."

Ramona brushed Blake's shoulder as she passed by her, and Blake ran out the door. My mom entered the floor as Blake ran into it. She chased her down to the ground floor.

The police came up shortly afterward, and Ramona tried to talk her way out of getting arrested for trespassing.

"She stole my keys. God only knows what else she stole off me." They questioned her and went through her purse. They found drugs and a load of cash. I looked and saw a pair of my personalized cufflinks in her purse. They had her, and she left in handcuffs.

I had to stay with the cops for questioning. All my thoughts were with where Blake could be. What she must be thinking. No signs of my mom either. Someone posted bail for Ramona in the morning, and I requested a restraining order against her.

My mom came back to my apartment after they took Ramona away.

"Mom, did you find her? Where is she?" I frantically fumbled for my phone to call Blake and she stopped me in my tracks.

"Maximo, stop. Please stop. Sit down. Blake is okay. She is in my apartment and doesn't want to see you right now. She's scared and confused. I told her that the police are here, and she saw some in the lobby. The doorman also confirmed that Ramona was not authorized. Calm down; she has calmed down. I want to hear what happened. I'm going to take the police report down to her to prove it. Okay? I told her about what she was doing to you, and she's just trying to process it all. But she's here and not going to flee."

"Okay, please tell her I love her and to come up here. I don't want to waste another minute. Please!" I was crying; I felt so foolish. I had a night of weakness, and now I may lose my Blake. The one minute she decides to come and see me, and I have this happen!

"Maximo, I will. We'll be in touch. Just try to relax." She left, and I dropped to my knees to pray as I cried like a child.

"Please Jesus, please. I love Blake; I promise I did everything I could to not hurt Ramona. Oh, man. Please forgive me. Help me get my Blake back. Please God, please." My tears were uncontrollable. I couldn't breathe. It hurt so bad. I was gasping for air. I didn't hear the door open. I didn't see Blake come in. But she came in and ran straight to me. Blake took my body and held it as I was convulsing. I wanted to tell her that I loved her, but my body took over and held me from speaking.

"Maximo, feel me, Maximo. Feel my body and start to follow my breathing. Follow my count, breathe in and out Maximo. You're going to be okay. Deep in one, two, three, deep out one, two, three, four. Okay, baby, you're getting better." We did this exercise a few times, and my body relaxed on her chest. She never let go. I was crying so hard my face was red and blotchy. I was embarrassed to look at her.

"Blake, I love you so much."

"Maximo, I love you so much." She made me cry again. I didn't stop. She didn't let go of me.

"Don't leave me ever again," I pleaded. "Don't leave me ever again."

"Maximo, I remember everything. I remember you. I remember the shore house and dating you. How could I ever have forgotten you? It was you, Maximo, it always was. I don't want to lose you again."

I lifted my blotchy tear-filled face to look into her eyes. She was smiling; her eyes were red as well. I kissed her as deeply as I could. We cried ourselves to sleep. I can never let go of her.

At four am we woke up to follow Blake's routine. We did it in silence; I let her take the lead. Her eyes had their sparkle back. I felt it when she looked at me. Once we finished, she came to curl into me in the bed. I drifted into a dream of Blake running through the field, signaling to me to chase her. She kept looking back, and I was still following her. This time I was able to catch her as we fell into the field of growing crops that cushioned our fall. She laughed as we hit the ground, and I laughed with her.

"I will always be here to catch you, Blake."

"I will always be here to catch you, Maximo." I heard kids running behind us, and we waited for them to come closer to us.

Her kisses woke me up from my dream. "Thank you, Maximo," she said. I think we were in the same dream.

"Let's not dream alone anymore, Blake."

"Yes, Maximo. I'll listen to you from now on." We kissed again. It was the morning I wanted to have for the rest of my life.

"Oh yeah, hey Blake. Thanks for visiting, so here's my place. You've already visited the bedroom. Let me take you on a tour."

We laughed as I lifted her out of bed. We held hands and I walked her through the rooms, kissing her the whole way in between laughing. She made me feel alive again.

"Oh, wait, we're in the bedroom again. How did that happen? Did you trick me into bringing you back here? Sneaky girl." We laughed, and she held her hands as high up to my neck as she could. I could not resist dipping down to kiss her.

"This time is for real, Maximo; I'm not turning back. You're stuck with me."

"Really, who says I want you to stick around?" We dazzled into a slow dance in between the conversation and kisses.

"Maximo, I came here to be with you. I want to be your wife, Maximo. I don't want to let you go. So, I came here to make sure you still felt the same for me. After last night I believe that you love me too. I hope that you still do."

"Blake, I never stopped."

"Good, so who was that crazy bitch?" We laughed again, and Blake dipped herself back as I soaked in her neck. I laughed so hard I couldn't catch my breath.

"Yeah, Blake, that's what happens when you leave me off on my own. So, stop doing that please."

"OMG Maximo, that was a little crazy."

"So, what happened? I had no idea that you were coming here. How did you find me?"

"Mazzy. I met up with Mazzy last week. She found me at a gallery opening. She told me that she promised to help you get me back. She gave me this picture of us. I didn't even recognize it. She told me that you were real in your love for me. She told me things about my fiancé that I wasn't aware of. So, I went to find the box that I never opened from my past. I found your flannel, your hat, and all the pictures of us. Maximo, I remembered you! I remembered us. I felt us. I don't want that to end. I was so ridiculous to not look at it sooner. I should have listened to you. I kept thinking someone was out to get me, and I fell for it. This jerk Ben tried to pull a scam on me. Mazzy did an investigation, and it turned out to be true. I had them serve him with papers to get out of my life, and I came here to see you."

"Blake, nice to mention you're engaged?"

"Maximo, I was so stupid. He lied and manipulated me. He really did. I fell under his spell. Please forgive me. I gave back the ring with a note stating that it's over. He turned out to be a horrible person, Maximo. We both made mistakes. We both found each other again. Can we stop playing this game? Please?" I walked away from her into the other room to sit on the couch and absorb the moment. She came to sit next to me and reached out for my hand and went down to her knees before me.

"Maximo, I am asking for forgiveness and to start over with you. I don't want to go back to being confused or trying to figure it out. I figured it out. I want to be with you because I love you, Maximo. I know it was you who saved me. I screamed for you. The police report confirmed that I was screaming out for Maximo. You saved me, Maximo. I am so grateful."

"I know that I'm not crazy. No turning back, Pumpkin. Are you sure now this is what you want to do?"

"Yes, Maximo. You're the only man in my heart. "

"Alright then."

CHAPTER THIRTY-THREE

~

We traveled back and forth on the weekends between Chicago and Miami. Sometimes we met at a middle location. Miami wore out its welcome. Blake wanted to wash herself of Chicago. The most natural place for us was to go back to New York.

Our last weekend in Chicago was for Mazzy and Zac's wedding, and we were in the wedding party. As Mazzy and Zac said their vows, I talked to Blake from across the altar by mouthing the words.

"That's us next."

"What?"

"I'm going to marry you, Blake."

"What?"

I widened my eyes as big as I could to get her to understand. It just made her laugh. I blew her a kiss. Blake blushed and looked to the side ceiling. She did that when she pretended to ignore me and didn't want to laugh because whatever I said was probably inappropriate. Then I laughed. The priest asked me to stop, as I was making a scene. Then the whole church laughed. I looked at Blake again and she at me, and the laughs came back.

"Young man, what's so funny that I have to stop this ceremony to ask."

"Forgive me, Father. I don't mean to upset or distract this wedding. We're all having a good time. We are all having a good time, right?" I asked out to the crowd, and they cheered and laughed. I think some crazy uncle whistled. Mazzy and Zac laughed too. The energy on that stage was good.

"So, Father, please understand that all I was simply mouthing to this beautiful lady right here is that we are going to be the next to get married. She was pretending not to hear me. So, I have to laugh. You can relate, right?" Again, I questioned the crowd, which also got a laugh.

"So, what is your name, son?"

"Maximo. And this beauty is Blake. The love of my life." The crowd awed us, and I egged them on.

"So, are you trying to propose to her right now at your friend's wedding?"

"OMG, please, please! Do it, do it!" Mazzy chanted to us with a little jump.

"Oh, no. She didn't hear me. She can wait. Please carry on. It's not about us after all." The church laughed, Blake blushed and laughed harder than anyone. The priest gave his disapproval, but he laughed too. Then the ceremony went on all the way to the I do's, and we walked back down the aisle into a storm of bubbles.

The ceremony was at a swanky hall in Chicago. We ruled the cocktail party together. As Zac didn't want all the attention, I had no problem with it. When it was time for our entrance, Blake and I had a routine that we practiced moments before we went out to the dance floor. I ended by getting on one knee and kissing her hand. The crowd cheered and awed. She laughed at the tease. Blake will have to wait for the real proposal.

We danced the night away. I grabbed as many people as I could for shots. I danced with both grandmas. Blake and I were back as the party couple, the couple everyone wanted to know about, and everyone will remember as the crazy ones from Mazzy's and Zac's wedding. I'm so glad to be back into this headspace. I'm so glad to be back with Blake.

I took her back out to the deck after the cake was cut. She wore my jacket on this chilly night, and we shared a drink as I wrapped her in my arms.

"Maximo, when I saw you for the first time again, you entered the room and had your eyes on me. I was the most important person in the room. I felt like that tonight. I feel like that every time I see you. I love it, Maximo. I really do."

"I'm glad. Because when I walk into a room, you are the only person I want to see. Oh Blake, what you do to me!" I turned her around to face me in my arms. We smiled, and she leaned into my chest. I rubbed her back.

"Hey girl, can you get my phone out of my pocket so that we can take a picture of us?" She went into the inside pocket and grabbed my phone, and I took a selfie of us.

"So, I just wanted to have a before and after."

"Before and after? Oh, of us tonight? I bet I look like a wreck. Or of us from when we met again at Jax's wedding?" I smiled as she rambled on.

"No, Pumpkin." I felt into the side pockets of my jacket she was wearing and took out the pouch with an engagement ring in it.

"No, pumpkin, one of us before we are engaged and one afterward. I want you to see how much happier I can make you. Ms. Blake, will you marry me?"

"What? OMG! Maximo, I want nothing more than to be your wife. You are so crazy. OMG!" I took another selfie with her in happy tears and showed her both.

"You are right, Maximo, each day I am with you is happier than the next. I love you so much." I kissed her and walked her into the reception and looked over for Zac and Mazzy. She caught eyes and saw the happy expression on our faces. Mazzy ran to the mic to announce that we had just gotten engaged. She was as happy for us as her wedding.

"Mazzy, I don't want to take away from your special day!"

"This is my special day that I would not have if Maximo hadn't come to chase after you and then meet me. He gave me the courage to get to Zac. I was destined to meet you guys to get to him. He met me to get to you. It's all destiny. I'm so happy to share this moment with you. Besides, at your wedding, I'm going to announce that I'm pregnant." They laughed and hugged. Our circle was formed. Blake will be my wife. Life was perfect.

CHAPTER THIRTY-FOUR

~

I packed up my office in Miami and started our first office in New York. I could not have dreamed of such an opportunity. Everything was coming together. Blake and I rented a place in the city until her house in Larchmont would be available for us to move into. We ate late dinners downtown and walked through Central Park. She took me to galleries that I had no idea what I was looking at. We ate hot dogs and drank beer at Yankee games. She accompanied me to client dinners and drew in business. She was my best asset. We were back to our show. We told stories across the dinner table and finished each other's sentences. We were the team I wanted. At dinner I mouthed to her across the table "I love you." She looked to the side ceiling. I knew she could hear me.

The Christmas season was back. We traveled down to Miami to be with my mom, and I had some meetings to attend in the home office. My mom, as always, went crazy on the holiday decorations and cooking. This year Blake joined in on the dancing and singing as we cooked. I love how my mom embraced her. The dinner this year is small. After the Ramona debacle, my mom kept her distance from some of her former friends. Her boyfriend came over and a few others. It was still fun and lasted way into the late-night hours. It was a perfect Christmas.

I went into the office excited by the progress we'd been accomplishing in New York. I met with the heads of the firm in a special meeting that was asked to be kept private. I was under the impression it was to congratulate me on the hard work and business growth.

"Nice work, Maximo. New York is going well. You kept your connections to your clients and brought the business to where it is exceeding our expectations. Very impressive. You seem very happy there."

"Thank you, gentleman. Yes, I love it in New York. I worked with our clients and kept some good relationships. I don't know, it just seems to flow. I couldn't be happier."

"Great, so we have some questions. Just routine, you know the business." He signaled to the outside to bring someone else in.

"Maximo, this is Fred, he's with the FBI and has some questions that we were flagged on some suspicious activity on some accounts. I'm sure you will be fine." I was nervous. What was suspicious? What had gone wrong? I run a legit business.

"Of course, Whatever you need to know." I answered all the questions on my clients and sent them files as needed. I was nervous. The FBI can make anybody nervous. They collected all the information they needed, and Fred was very nice but with no sense of humor. I made it through the day. My bosses said to just conduct business as usual and if they had anything they would let me know. I went home a bit shaky. I came to find my mom and Blake laughing on the deck. I poured myself a scotch and entered their conversation.

"Hi, Maximo. How was your day? You look kind of pale, Hon. You okay?" I was a ghost white that I could feel. The scotch hit me quickly.

"Just jealous the party started before I got here. It looks like you ladies are having a good time. Nice." I did my best to deflect the conversation.

I was quiet for most of the evening. Blake and my mom caught on that something was wrong with me. When I excused myself to head into the bedroom, Blake followed. I undressed and went straight into bed and turned on the TV. She came into the bed, still moisturizing her hands, and went right into my side where she found her spot.

"Talk to me, Maximo. I know you're upset about something."

"Yeah, I need time to process. The FBI came in today and asked me a thousand questions about all my clients and went through all my files. It was scary. They told me just to conduct business as usual. If they find something, they'll let me know. I'm not doing anything wrong, but I'm freaked out."

"Maximo! OMG. I would be freaked out too. But I also believe that most companies with access to all this high profile confidential information get questioned on stuff? Maybe it's nothing to worry about. I watch you do business, Maximo. I don't see anything shady going on. Maybe you should talk to Mazzy?"

"She's away on her honeymoon. They couldn't leave until they both had cleared their schedules. I don't want to bother her unless it's necessary. I'll wait to hear something and then talk to her."

"Maximo! Give her a heads-up and call her. I'm sure she can understand the severity of your feelings. You guys are more than friends—you trust her and I trust her!"

"Alright, pumpkin, I'll call her in the morning. Right now, I want some Blake time." I distracted her with kisses and turned off the TV.

We left Miami, and I didn't call Mazzy. I brushed it under the rug and left it there. I went about my ways and continued to do business. I was not directed to do anything else. Blake and I set a date to get married and have it small enough to hold the reception in our home. I focused on that.

We finally moved into our house. It was still outdated from when she lived here so many years ago, but we didn't have the time to redecorate and make the house ours before our wedding. The wedding was planned for just a few weeks away. Blake was not nervous; I was a mess. I just wanted to be married already. We didn't need a wedding to prove our love for each other. We waited so long for this. One early morning a knock came on our door. We were not expecting anything. Blake went to answer, and it was two FBI agents that greeted her. She was in shock. They had a warrant under my name to search our house. She let them in and called Mazzy right away.

"Mazzy, the FBI is here searching our house. I don't know what's going on. Did Maximo talk to you?"

"No, Blake, about what?"

"OMG, he got questioned by the FBI around Christmas, I told him to call you. He didn't really?"

"No, Blake. I'm on the next plane down there. Don't answer anything until I get there."

"Okay, thank you, Mazzy."

"Maximo! Maximo!" It was too late; they already found me upstairs. She ran up to see me.

"Maximo, what's going on? I called Mazzy, and she's on her way. She said not to answer anything."

"Okay, Blake, okay. Relax. We didn't do anything wrong; there's nothing to hide. It's okay." She ran into me for comfort.

"Madam, I know this is scary, but we have to look into some suspicious activity and need you and your husband to come to our offices. This is a search based on some suspicious calls we received on your husband's business. I know that you're waiting on your lawyer, and you can have her meet you there.

"She's coming from Chicago."

"Okay, well then you'll have to wait for her there."

"Maximo?"

"Alright, whatever you need for us to do. Mazzy will meet us there. Blake, it's okay. We have no reason to be alarmed." I calmed her down. We went to the station to wait in a blank, quiet room. After five hours, Mazzy arrived. Mazzy was able to get some information and do research while she was on the plane. It turns out that someone was in my files and stole some identities from them and turned them around to play us and use the fraudulent money to reinvest in our New York Office. They seemed to think I was in on this.

"Oh gosh, Mazzy, what? Who?"

"Maximo, think of anyone who would have unauthorized access into your accounts?"

"I don't know. It could be anyone in my office. There's also Ramona. Ramona went into my office a bunch of times. I mean I have no idea what was on my desk and what she saw. She's a con-artist."

"That can be it. Answer all their questions; I'll be right there with you." We went through questioning and were released after several hours. Mazzy came back with us to the house.

"So, what do we do next?" I asked, scared to death.

"Maximo. I don't think they have anything on you but be prepared. Identity theft is big, and this is a serious crime. Whoever did this will go to jail for a long time. I'll work on gaining access to a video of her in your office. Right now, do business as usual and keep a low profile. Don't travel anywhere."

"Should we cancel the wedding?"

"No, that will look suspicious. Conduct business as usual. Be prepared that you could be asked to postpone the honeymoon."

"Alright. Thank you, Mazzy." When we went to bed, Blake and I talked about the wedding.

"Maximo. Do you think Ramona has something to do with this?"

"Blake, she got herself into my apartment by her manipulation. She got herself into my office through manipulation. I can't imagine what else she did to me, and I don't even know it. Damn it. Blake, I'm so sorry you're involved in this mess. I'm so upset."

"Maximo, we're in this together forever. I know Mazzy said not to do anything off the radar. I want to get married. Let's go to the priest in the morning, explain what's going on, and ask him to marry us privately, just in case."

"In case? Oh man, Blake, I'm freaking out. I want nothing to get in the way of this wedding. Let's do it."

That morning we went to the priest and told him our story and our fears. He married us in a private ceremony in the chapel. We followed up with the marriage certificate as it was time to pick it up. Thankfully we did so.

We went to the chapel with the priest and a few witnesses as necessary. I was able to say I love you in front of God and made it official. I held my hands on her face as our foreheads touched each other. We both cried—the moment was so sacred.

The day before the actual wedding, I was arrested at my job for identity and investment fraud. I was sent to a holding jail before the trial. Since I had a record already, and Blake had lots of cash and connections here and overseas, they felt I was a flight risk. We canceled the wedding, and I spent the night in jail along with the next night and the night after that. It was a horrible somber time here. It was nights without Blake.

I love you, my Blake. Please don't give up on me.

I love you, Maximo; I'm never giving up on you. Never.

CHAPTER THIRTY-FIVE

~

I don't look good in orange. Does anyone? I was once told that orange is the color of deceit. I was taken advantage of. How did I get here? I became cattle. I lost my identity. I was a nobody. I had trouble seeing; my glasses were at home. I couldn't have visitors just yet. I was waiting for Mazzy to come, give me updates, and bring me certain approved items like my glasses and a picture of myself and Blake. All I felt was missing Blake. It was as if I felt us die. Was I dead? I felt dead. I had just got my Blake back and suddenly we're torn apart.

I found myself a loner here. I didn't want to get comfortable or make friends. A guy named Charlie came to sit with me a few times. I didn't get to see where he was coming from. He wasn't on my side of the cellblock. He somehow was able to move about and sit where he wanted, when most of us had to stick to certain areas. He was kind of like a prison "godfather" of sorts. He was called Uncle Buddy by another gentleman. They all had a quite nice group—very smart and put together. They were of all ethnicities. Uncle Buddy was an older black man from Brooklyn. They all were reformed in some way and very respectful to others. Not what I expected to find. Somehow they found me. Nice to know not everyone is a hardcore blood-related criminal.

Uncle Buddy became a friend. I was able to go for walks with him on the grounds when it wasn't my allotted time. He seemed to have some pull around the place. I went with it because he made me feel so comfortable.

It was weird; he was always around when I needed someone to talk to. He knew when to show up. I appreciated his friendship. Uncle Buddy put me in a good mindset and told me how to stay positive. He really had me turn to God. I forgot that God existed, especially now. I relied on holidays and quick prayers and then put God back on a shelf. He needed to be put into my pocket and into my heart. Uncle Buddy really showed me how important God was in my life. I was in jail, but so grateful for all the things I have. Especially Blake. I could not be strong without my Blake.

So, I kept at my task at hand. I worked on staying positive like Uncle Buddy taught me. I tried to look at the spiritual side of it all. If I were being taught a lesson, what was it? Am I going crazy? There's too much silence in this place. The echoes hurt my ears during the nighttime when someone screamed. I still wake up at four am.

"Morning, my Blake. I love you. I'm coming home soon. I promise, my love.

I believe, my love. I believe."

Mazzy brought down her best team to work on my case. Blake sat in on all the meetings and strategies. They worked day and night about what could go wrong during the trial and worked on angles for all the due diligence they received. There were a few avenues where they could prove that I was being framed from the footage of who came in and out of the office. Ramona was found leaving the office with a paper in her hand. Maybe she stole information? When she was in the apartment, maybe she went through my private computer? Could she have gotten into my phone? They questioned all of it. When Mazzy was in a good place and ready for my part, she came for a meeting.

Mazzy entered the small room with a mirrored window. She had my glasses and the pictures I requested. That was all I wanted. We went through all the video footage and questions. The paper Ramona took was after she asked me to write down the address of a restaurant. I didn't question why she was asking, I just wanted her to leave. It could have very much had private information on the other side. It was a lead. Why would she need an address from me? She grew up in Miami, how would I know better than her where something was? Mazzy's team went to investigate it further. We went through encounters and every connection we could. The trial date was so far away. Each minute in here felt like a year. I missed Blake so.

"Maximo, we're going to get you out of here. I know it," Mazzy said as she touched my hand.

"This sucks, Mazzy. I don't get it. Why is someone out to get me? What did I do so wrong here?"

"I don't know. But Maximo, I am not giving up. Blake is so help-ful—she loves you."

"I know. It sucks in here."

"I know, Maximo. I know. Blake told me to tell you to just breathe. Listen for her and how she taught you to breathe. You can do it. She also said to tell you never to stop four am and that you'll know what that means."

Tears streamed down my face. "Mazzy, this means everything. Everything. Thank you so much. I know and believe you'll get me out of here."

We closed for the day. I was in there for months. It was a difficult time in my life. I stayed as strong in gratitude as I possibly could. Uncle Buddy kept me on track with that. I hardly spoke to anyone but Uncle Buddy and some others in his crew. They were amazing to me. I was kind to the officers; I found that made them be nice to you. I went to Mass with my crew and we spoke and prayed together as a group every day. They made this hard time in here worth it. I could not have done it without them.

"Always believe in God. He never gives up on you and always for-gives. Always," Uncle Buddy said. In one of our walks, he told me his story. He'd been in and out of here since he was a teenager. He was now in his sixties. The crew he hung with were all connected through the years. Their stories were similar. They had become a family while they were in prison. They were at peace in there, which is hard to do.

Uncle Buddy stayed out of trouble and they all had families that they prayed for every day. I joined them. I prayed for Blake, my mom, Nico, and my dad and his children. Uncle Buddy told me to pray for all the people who ever hurt me. I prayed for my dad, I prayed for Rachel, I prayed for Barbara, I prayed for Ramona, and I prayed for Ben. He stole Blake from me. I prayed and prayed. It made me feel good. My time was becoming therapeutic. This group gave me something that I was lacking — to see that I needed God. I needed Him more than ever in good times and in bad. I thanked Him for my path and how it led me to Blake. She saved me every time. I know she'll save me again. I'll save her again. It was four am.

"I love you, Blake. I'll be home soon, my love. I will."

"I need you, Maximo. Please hurry."

My mom came up to stay with Blake and get ready for the trial. Everyone was nervous about how it would turn out. I stayed in faith and concentrated on seeing myself with Blake on the couch, sitting by the fire as I sketched her. I know I will have that day again. I know it.

"Blake, I have something for you. It is Maximo's. Well, I took it from his stuff before he moved back to New York since not everything was going to fit into your place. I know he would want you to have this."

She handed Blake my first sketch of her before I even knew her. Her hair the exact same way she wears it now. Her eyes in detail. I sketched that before I met her. She never saw it. She never knew that I was about to be an artist. It was dated 1989. I didn't meet Blake until 1991. My mom had it framed for her to keep as a gift of hope.

"Maria, this is so beautiful. OMG, who drew this?"

"Oh, Blake. Oh, Blake. I wanted you to have this for a reason. Oh, my Maximo is my favorite person on this earth. I love Nico too, don't get me wrong. But Maximo was my first love. I came to America because I saw him in my dreams. He was in my heart. I wanted a life for him, I dreamed of America of where to find him. Maximo has dreams in his heart. He dreamt of you before he knew you. He drew you before he knew you. This is the first sketch. I want you to have it to know that he always had hope for you in his heart. I know that God is doing this to bring you closer, not further apart. He needs your love and support. Not that I don't think you aren't giving him that. I just want you to have faith. To show you the promise God gave him. It will all be okay."

Blake was awestruck by the sketch and how much it did look like her.

"I love you, Maximo, I love you. Come home, baby. I'm waiting for you."

"I know, pumpkin, I know," I replied to her voice in my head.

CHAPTER THIRTY-SIX

~

The morning of the trial came and all of us were nervous. It would be the first time I would see Blake in months or my mom, or any of my family for that matter. Mazzy brought me a suit.

"Be strong, we got this," she said to me before we walked out into the courtroom. I just wanted to see Blake and my mom. I missed everyone so much. They opened the door to the courtroom, and it was full of friends and family. I had support—people who believed in me. My dad was there, my mom, Nico. Then my Blake. Her face was swollen but glowing. I looked into her eyes as she held in her tears the best she could. I looked at her to take her in. I missed her beauty.

I looked down and saw her stomach—a perfectly round belly. Blake was pregnant. My tears came down. I was able to be close enough to touch her and hug her. No one objected.

"I need you to come home, pumpkin. We need you," she whispered in my ear.

It was my motivation. I had to get home as soon as possible. I gathered myself together as I listened to her breathing behind me. The room needed to collect themselves together as they recognized I had not known she was pregnant.

"Order, order!" the judge demanded from the crowd.

The day was long. The next day longer. Then the next. I was beat, and some days I went straight to sleep from all the stress. We were making progress, but was it enough? I know there is something we should pinpoint, but what?

Uncle Buddy came to visit me one night to see how I was feeling. We chatted for a bit, and he made me feel better that it would come together as long as I believed. He told me that he used to live in Chicago once upon a time. He was at one point in between jail stints and worked at a law firm as part of his services. He told me he was watching my trial on the internet and asked me about Blake. He asked me about Blake's relationship with Ben. He knew of a case where Ben was involved with investment fraud and was able to get out of it because of the law firm he worked at. There was our window.

"Uncle Buddy, can you get information about that? How was it not in their information?"

"Oh yeah, he paid people off and changed his identity. Back then you could get away with it. I'll get you all the information. See, God is good. This may be your avenue to get out of here."

"Uncle Buddy, you're amazing! I'm so grateful." We hugged.

"Yeah, we need to get you out of here. It looks like your wife is due soon. You need to be there for the birth."

"Uncle Buddy, you are a godsend. You really are. How does such a great guy like yourself get into jail?"

"Easy, I need a break from my wife. I also need to meet someone like yourself to help me believe that God puts us in situations for a reason." He left laughing as he walked away.

"Oh Jesus, You're amazing. I'm listening. Help guide me to get home to Blake. I want to be there before my baby is born. Thank You, Jesus."

Four am came around. I woke right up without even checking.

"Blake, my love, I found a way to get me home to you and our baby. I'm coming home. Please wait to give birth until then."

"I love it. I can't wait. I miss you, pumpkin. Come home soon."

CHAPTER THIRTY-SEVEN

～

The morning routine was the same. Buses to the court, and my suit waiting for me there. I changed and had a few moments to meet with Mazzy before we entered the courtroom. Mazzy came in smiling with excitement.

"Well, well, Maximo. I have amazing news. I got a call last night with some information about Ben. It turns out that he was involved in an identity and investment fraud before, paid off the judges, and was given an all-new identity, and so the old was wiped off his record. My team was able to link him to Ramona, and we have proof that they're framing you. We got this, Maximo!"

"OMG Mazzy! Uncle Buddy. He told me all this last night. He did this; he's amazing!"

"I don't know who that is, and I can't reveal where the information came from. But someone is looking out for you for sure."

I hugged Mazzy right as we were about to walk into the courtroom. Mazzy asked the Judge if she could approach the bench and revealed all the new information she was able to uncover along with the documentation. The judge sent both lawyers back to their seats and looked through the documents just as a squeamish scream came from behind me. It was Blake. She was turning red and screamed out in pain. I went to reach for her and was held back by the court officer. The judge ordered EMS to come, and my mom and dad escorted her out of the room. I teared up as I was not able to move. I could not help my Blake.

"Blake, I love you. Wait for me to have this baby. I want to be there. Please wait for me"

"Order, order!" The judge demanded. He was upset. "Legal, both of you in my chambers. We'll take a twenty-minute recess." The gavel slammed; we all went to our corners. I took this silent time to pray for Blake and my baby, for Uncle Buddy, and for Mazzy and her wondrous works. Then the doors opened. We all stood for the judge. I was asked to remain standing for the next piece of information. The judge came back to the courtroom.

"Maximo Cruz, there has been significant information to lead me to see you're not guilty of this crime, and this is now deemed a mistrial. I'm ordering the summons of Ben XXX and Ramona XXX for the crime of Identity and Investment fraud in this case. Mr. Cruz, you're free to go. Now please get him processed ASAP to get him to his wife who is in labor. No reason why this man should spend another moment away from his family than he already has. The gavel slammed again, and the harmonious sound rang. I hugged Mazzy quickly as she also wanted me to race to Blake. They took me back to my cell to retrieve my personal items and then to processing.

"Where is Uncle Buddy? Where is he? I have to thank him!" I asked my assigned officer.

"Maximo, I don't know who that is." I gave him the description, and he still didn't know. I asked the guy next to me, and he shrugged his shoulders. He was a mirage.

"Thank you, Uncle Buddy. Wherever you are. You are for sure another angel in my life."

My paperwork was pushed through, and everyone cheered me on. It was such excitement with high fives and hugs, although it was somewhat bittersweet. I didn't even know I existed while I was here. But now I knew that I had all this support. Who knew that these people would watch over me? I'll pray for all of them. I cried on my way. It was an amazing experience. Even the guards were excited and in amazement. I didn't think an experience in jail could be like this. When we opened the doors, I soaked in the air and sunshine. It was time to see Blake. Mazzy waited for me right at the front doors, and we had a police escort requested by the judge to go to the hospital. I can see how God is good, how being dedicated to him and staying in faith pays off. I am so grateful.

We made it through the doors, and I was put into proper scrubs and sent into the delivery room just in time. Blake was pushing, and my mom was there with her. I held her other hand just in time to see the head popping through. A few more pushes and then our son Chaz was born. He was skinny and long—nothing like me. Ha! Everything like me. But he was sweet like Blake. They cleaned him up and checked him out before handing him to us. Blake took him while I admired the two of them together. God always gives us blessings.

We went back to the room to be alone with our Chaz.

"Oh, hey, pumpkin. Thanks for waiting for me," I said as I held Chaz in my arms.

"You're still an ass. I missed you so much." I came in to kiss her and handed Chaz back to her.

"We can't take any more time apart, my love. No more." I kissed them both. I didn't want to stop.

"Then stop going on these crazy cult retreats where you wear all orange and smell funny." She was still a wit.

"Alright, Momma has spoken. Did you hear that, Chaz? Your momma makes lots of demands. Get used to it," I said, talking to my son. I have a son! I can't believe it. My life is the most amazing gift. I slept on the futon next to Blake and at four am my eyes opened. I waited for Blake. She awoke five minutes later. She looked up for Chaz. Once she saw him sleeping soundly, she looked for me.

"You're late," I said to her. She smiled as she tried to get herself up. I helped her to the bathroom and back to bed with her water. Chaz squirmed and moved about. I couldn't resist. I picked him up and walked around with him.

"Hi, buddy. I'm going to call you buddy like Uncle Buddy. He got me back to you. His real name is Charlie. So, we named you Chaz—short for Charlie. So, we always remember the blessing he gave us. Never underestimate the power of God. Never."

As I danced with Chaz, Blake looked over and watched us. She couldn't keep her eyes open. But she smiled and was content. I held my promise to be there for the birth. I looked into Chaz's eyes as he tried to open them and say something. He couldn't yet.

I held him close and looked out the window. My thoughts drifted. I saw the FBI come to Ben's house. The search. Finding the evidence. The arrest. Then the FBI banging on Ramona's door and her laying topless on her deck, smoking pot. The FBI welcomed the search to find drugs and evidence of her link to Ben. The arrest. The arraignment. The sentencing of a long time in jail. All for jealousy. All for greed. Uncle Buddy told me once that the only time Jesus showed anger was when something was tied to money and greed. I pray for their souls. I remember my dad telling me how money can ruin you. It sure ruined them. I'm sad for greedy people. I'm so grateful for my new life. Only God could be this good to me.

CHAPTER THIRTY-EIGHT

~

We took Chaz home. Blake had used the time when I was away to decorate and make the home ours. I didn't feel at home yet. It was hard for me to adjust to being free. It also had been hard to sit in a jail cell without my loved ones around me. I had a hard time adjusting and didn't want to show it. I stayed in faith, but this was hard. We got back together, and then we were torn apart. We began to relearn each other and our new addition at the same time. Having everything I had wanted and fought so long to get was a new experience. Now I had it. I was nervous that I didn't know what to do with it. Sometimes the good emotions are harder to deal with than the bad ones. The bad ones were so frequent and easy. I hoped I didn't mess it up.

Blake hung my sketch I drew of her before I knew her in the entrance-way of our home. It was the place where it all started, where I dreamed of her, and we started our journey together before we ever met. She felt it should be the feeling you get when you entered our home.

At night we danced around the house, tossing Chaz between us for feedings and getting him to sleep. The house was hers and his. It wasn't mine yet. I felt a bit out of place. We danced around the house, singing to Chaz and rocking him to sleep. Blake loved to bring him to the sketch.

"Chaz, this is your daddy's sketch of when he dreamed about me back when he was a young kid and had no idea who I was. But he found me, Chaz. He did it. Now he has us. What do you think?" Chaz cooed, and Blake looked up to me with a smile.

"Maximo, why didn't I ever know that you used to be an artist?" Blake looked at me wanting to know.

"Oh, Blake. That's like a lifetime ago. Yeah, I dreamt of you in a field asking me to chase you."

"I have that dream. I am in a white dress running through a field and signaling someone to follow me. Well, now that you say that, I have that dream often. Wait, I had that dream when I was little. Maximo. I remember something!"

"Wow, we've had the same dream for all these years. And you couldn't remember me?" I was joking with her. She was tired and emotional. Bad timing.

"I guess not," she answered and handed Chaz to me as she went into the bedroom and closed the door. My mom came out of her bedroom just behind the living room.

"Maximo. She's full of hormones. Your sarcasm is not always the best medicine. Give me Chaz and go take care of that please!" my mom said to rescue me.

I walked up the stairs slowly, not all that sure of what I had done wrong. I was just making a joke; this was hard to understand for both of us. Blake sat out on our deck in a lounge chair with her arms folded into her sweater, looking tensely out into the yard. I know that she wants to remember things. She lived in this house for years and didn't remember it. I remember things about us and this house that upsets her not to know. It is hard not to know who you used to be. I wish I could forget. I came behind her and kissed the side of her neck softly as a peace offering and then moved to the adjoining chair.

"Blake, I'm sorry. I didn't mean to hurt your feelings. I know how upsetting it is for you to not remember things. All that matters is that we're together now, and we have Chaz. We'll have all new memories."

"Maximo, I'm not upset that I don't remember the past. I'm upset that I love this life so much, I don't want to remember the past. Like it would change everything. Maybe I don't want to remember for a reason?"

"Oh, that's interesting. I didn't think of it that way. Then don't go back there. Don't remember things you don't want to. Did you ever get hypnotized?"

"The doctors thought it might help. I didn't want to. It was as if I was fine with it somehow and wanted to move forward. I look out at this yard and think of Chaz running around. I also think of someone else running around back here. I see a little girl growing up here. I want to look into the future and not the past. I want to have another child, Maximo. I love our life as crazy as it has been. I want to keep it growing. I feel that my family is around me, but I don't remember them. I get glimpses, but I do feel love from them. I believe they are with us. I'm happy about that. I want to just keep it that way."

"I'm glad to hear you are at peace with your family. I agree, they are with us. Uncle Buddy showed me that there's always love surrounding us so I believe they are. Wow, another kid. Can we take a breather? I know that we're older. Feeling the pressure to have another is just a lot for me right now. I'm still adjusting to living here and having a baby, I had no idea about, learning who I am again, who you are again, who we are as a family. Another baby I would cherish, but I need to take this all in first."

"I understand, Maximo. She's coming if we like it or not. I can feel it. But Maximo, I do love this life and couldn't be happier. I'm worried that you are a tad uneasy. Maybe this is not what you wanted? Are you alright?" She always knew how to read me.

"Blake, I wanted you for so long all I knew was how to dream about you and chase you and then, be rejected. So, it's sometimes hard to get what you want—hard to accept it and learn to love it. I learned to live in an upset for so long. It's hard to adjust to such happiness. But I want the happiness. I do." We sat silently after that.

"I never wanted to hurt you, Maximo, never."

"I know Blake. I was hurt. We're past that."

"When you were in jail, I did everything I could to make this house ours. I wanted you to come home and feel warm and loved. Do you feel that?"

"I do, Blake. I'm just adjusting. I know you did everything to make this ours. I just need time to feel it. I don't know what my future is going to be. Do I go back to work? Do I get a new job? Can I get a new job? Can I provide for us? I have new worries. I love how you decorated this house. You're such a natural at being a mom, but I don't feel adequate at being a dad. I worry if I'll adjust, and if I don't, will you reject me again? Will I frustrate you? I worry."

Blake came over to sit in my lap. I looked aside. I was hurting. I wanted to get to the happiness, but I was hurt. I'll always wonder if I'm enough or if she'll leave me when she unpeels the layers of who I am. These fears were so real. She held my face and kissed my cheek, working her way to my lips. She went in for a kiss, but I didn't react. I wanted to cry, but I can't let her see me cry. My face was getting red, and my breathing was short. She was too close to hide from.

"Maximo, Maximo. You can't disappoint me. I look at you every day and worry that I'm not enough for you. Can I be a good mom? Can I be a good wife? You know more about me than I do. I'm scared that not knowing my past makes me empty. Will I bore you? Will this life bore you and push you away? I worry too. I felt you. You told me to follow my heart, and it brought me to you. Now we have Chaz. I'm so happy. I have no intention of leaving you. You're stuck with me. I made a vow, a promise. I'm not backing down. I stood by you. I knew you were innocent. I believed in you. I hope that you can believe in me.

"As for work, Maximo, do what's in your heart. If you don't want to go back, then don't. If you want to start something else, then do that. I support you. We don't need the money. We are set for all that we need. I also like what I'm doing and will keep working. Maybe you should stay home and take care of Chaz. Would that bore you? Maybe you can go back to sketching. Perhaps that will help you get past your fears? Whatever you want, Maximo. I'm in this with you forever. I want you to know that."

I moved my face back to hers and felt her leaning on me. She always made me feel better. She went in for the kiss and I pushed her away. I wasn't mad at her, I was just confused. I thought this situation was about her feelings. I didn't realize they would be about mine. I was drained of all these emotions. I looked at her with sad eyes, and she understood. I just looked at her. . .really looked at her. She always is smiling. I saw my future in her and knew it would all be okay. But I was tired and needed to rest from all of this. I moved her off me and laid back on the bed, desperately needing sleep. Blake took off my shoes and my belt and then got me under the covers.

She stayed with me until I was off dreaming. I dreamed of us in the field. She was running, and I was chasing after her. We ran into the woods past the dark forest. We ran until we fell into the field. It was sunny. She laughed and grabbed me to twirl around in the weeds. Chaz is watching over us. A young girl is watching over us. They smiled, and Blake pointed to them. It was warming.

"I need to get past the forest, Blake. Help me get past the ugly darkness."

"Always, my love. Always."

Blake went downstairs to find my mom with Chaz sleeping in her arms. "I'm guilty, Blake," my mom said. "I can't resist him. I know you want him to sleep in his crib, but I'm going home soon. I want to soak in each moment. They grow up so fast." Blake sat next to them and cuddled with them to admire Chaz sleeping.

"He's irresistible. Just like his dad." They laughed softly not to wake him up. Blake brushed her fingers along his soft cheek, and he moved himself to feel it. They had a connection.

"So, Blake. How are you doing? Motherhood is not easy, especially for the first few months. You're lucky to have each other to take care of him. Most men are also a handful but not Maximo. He always stepped in when things got bad. When I had my miscarriage, my husband was out with another woman. Then he came back to tell me he was having a baby with her. I was crushed. Lost. Maximo took care of me. He's loving. I know he just upset you. He didn't mean any harm."

"He didn't upset me with his comments. I already knew he was a jerk. It's not a shock." My mom laughed at her.

"Alright then. Good to know. I think you'll be just fine then."

"So, Maria, can I ask? Was that the breaking point of your marriage? That moment? Was it ever good? I want some advice to keep my marriage together. I'm nervous. Maximo has so many fears about being happy. I want to make him feel comfortable. I want to make him feel safe with me."

"Well, my lady. It was a long way coming. I love Dario. I never stopped. We had challenges so that I maybe went in the wrong direction. I was lost when he left. Then he came back. I was afraid to lose him. I did many stupid things. But now I'm content. He has another woman. He has another child. He is happy now. He wasn't happy back then. We're better off as friends. Sometimes relationships have a shelf life. Sometimes they evolve, and you have to recognize that. We didn't evolve together. We evolved separately to try to be better for each other instead of being with each other and asking those questions of what would make the other happy. Listening to the signs. We didn't listen to our hearts at the right times.

"Don't worry to the point that it steals your joy. You're so con- nected. You talk to each other without words. I watched the both of you. You work as a team. Dario was not as helpful with Maximo when he was that age. You have a harmonious dance. You have a connection. Look at Chaz. He's peaceful because you bring him peace. Maximo needs your reassurance. He wanted you forever. Just remind him often that this is a gift. He's happy. He'll always be fighting for your attention. That's all he knows to do. Let him do it. It's okay to let someone love you and fight for it every day."

CHAPTER THIRTHY-NINE

~

I moped around the house for the next few days and stayed in the same clothes. No one gave in to my funk. I took time with Chaz and maybe was a bit overwhelming, hogging all the time with him. I needed the silence. He was becoming a bit of an obsession. Maybe I was going through postpartum depression. I was not who I wanted to be.

I thought so much of Uncle Buddy and how I wanted to talk to him right now. I needed a friend, someone I trusted. He was all I could think of. I went out into the yard with Chaz and spoke out loud to him. I hoped that he would hear me. I hoped that God was listening to me. I needed someone to talk to. I paced around the yard, and Chaz was sleeping soundly.

"Uncle Buddy, I love my wife. I don't want to disappoint my family. I don't know who I am anymore. Help me find who I am." There was no answer, but I saw a red cardinal that came flying through the trees and landed in my view. It stood there and looked right at me. The silence was extreme—it said something to me. I felt its presence. They say a cardinal is a sign of someone who comes to visit you from heaven. I thought of Blake's dad; even though I never met the man, I pictured it to be him. I don't know, maybe someone else. But that bird talked to me, and I knew it was going to be okay. I went back inside and was greeted by my mom.

"Maximo, I'm leaving tomorrow. Get out of this headspace. Don't make Blake crazy," Mom demanded as she cooked us one last dinner. I stood in my tracks on the stairs coming down from putting Chaz to bed. They both looked at me, and I looked back. It was the kick in the ass I needed. I went to shower, welcomed by Blake and a towel.

"Pumpkin, are you okay?"

I needed her. She helped dry me as I admired her. "Yes, I'm okay. I'm much better now that you're holding me. I hate being in these funks. I'm trying, baby. I don't know what got into me. I have everything to be grateful for."

"Maximo, I want you to be happy and feel safe here. I'm not going anywhere. Just let me in, okay? Let's enjoy the last night with your mom and have fun. You are fun, remember?" She held me close. How could I push off this affection?

"Alright. I can be fun. If you insist." She took the towel away from me and smirked as she left the room. I was forgiven.

We danced before dinner and drank wine. My mom turned up the music, Chaz sat in his chair and watched us, not sure of what was going on. Blake gave him her finger to hold as she danced with him, and he held onto it for dear life. We had added to our party.

After dinner, we retreated to sit by the fire and drink scotch, reminiscing over my mom's visit. I was going to have to say goodbye again to my best friend. Blake excused herself, giving us time alone. She understood the relationship we have.

CHAPTER FOURTY

~

Chaz was a few months old, and we were having much fun taking care of him together. I had to decide what I was going to do about work. The firm called to check in with a nudge that I had to decide soon. I needed to go back to doing something. I was not sure where I belonged anymore. The Miami team was coming to New York and requested to meet with me. I was happy to take a ride back into the city.

I entered the conference room full of suits. They all congratulated me on Chaz and asked how Blake was doing. There was no mention of the time I spent in jail or the lack of communication or support from them. I pushed it all behind me. They talked, and I didn't hear anything. The feeling of being in that office was cold. It was almost worse than being in a cell for all those months. I tried to look them all in the eye and they shied away, looked down, or looked to the next man for help. They couldn't look at me. Then the fake smiles came out with a proposal. I could stay at the firm and take on a new position they made just for me. I had a name now of how to run an ethical business, but that is not what they wanted. They wanted to use me to be the auction piece as they believed it would bring in more business. If I left, it would make them look bad. They needed me. I was set up.

I took a few minutes to soak in their words. It was all bullshit—it wasn't about the money, it wasn't about the drive of the job, it was about me. I needed to see this moment and take care of what was the right thing to do for me. I didn't need them. I had a family now; I had the woman I always wanted. I didn't need to be treated badly by anyone any longer. I was done. I could hear Blake in my head "*Maximo, do what you want to do. What you want to do. I will always support you.*"

I laughed a bit at the proposal they handed me—the extra zero at the end and the incentives. They were trying to buy my affection. It was sad. I didn't need any of this. My freedom, my time with my family, and my self-value were more important than numbers on a piece of paper. I laughed out loud, staring at this paper.

"Mr. Cruz, I believe that this offer is very generous. I think you can see you will be well taken care of," the suit said from across the room.

I looked him in the eye; he was the only one that looked back. He was the only one that didn't have a heart. The other faces looked down, ashamed and embarrassed that they wanted to use me to drive their numbers up, but they didn't care about me when I sat alone in a jail cell. They didn't believe me, but now they needed me. I didn't need them. I was done with being abused by people, taking a fall for something I didn't do. Nice guys finish last but not this time. I was ready to win and take charge of my life. I could see Blake laughing with Chaz playing. They were the ones there for me. They were who I wanted to fight for. I took the paper and slowly ripped it in half, then each piece again and again as I looked them in the face. All of them. I stood up and felt a relief of joy within me. The depression was gone. The anxiety was gone. I was ready for happiness.

"Gentleman, I know that all of you have a child at home. Some of you have several. How do you think I felt spending months in jail being accused of something I didn't do? I knew I was framed and that maybe no one in this room had a hand in it. Maybe someone in this room did. I will never know. I don't need to. You all worked with me and know that I am a good person and that I always ran an ethical, legit business. You all turned your backs on me and handed me over to the FBI. I know what you did. All of you. Ron—you went and moved all your money into a private account at another bank. Mikey—you went and put your money in your wife's name at a private bank down the street. Paul—you took your money and bought assets in your girlfriend's name, not your wife's. You all acted guilty of something, and guess what I did? I sat in a jail cell alone while my wife that I almost lost was home pregnant with my son.

"I prayed and prayed that the truth would be found and told. I stayed in truth because I live my life by being an honest, good-hearted person. You know what? That gave me everything I need. I got the woman I have loved to marry me. She had my child that I love more than life. I was found not guilty, and it was counted as a mistrial because I hadn't done anything wrong. I have everything I want because I believed in God and I believed in myself. Not one of you can even look me in the eye. So, your 'proposal' is shit. It's a guilty way to say 'Oh, my bad. Sorry, bro. Thanks for hanging in there.' I don't want your blood money. So, consider this my resignation."

I threw the ripped pages in the air and pulled books and piles of paper on the floor as I walked out the door with a dramatic exit. It was the most liberating feeling I have had in my life. I felt alive. The elevator door closed, and I laughed in tears as it went down. I hoped to never see those people again.

I decided to walk around the city for a bit to soak up what just happened and found myself in a park where I used to eat lunch on nice days. The air was still cold since it was still winter, but it had stopped snowing. It changed the feeling of what cold was. I sat with the anxious feelings consuming me and I sat waiting for them to leave my body slowly as a tremble does right after a big earthquake. What did I just do? The waves were leaving my body. I started to feel weak, then exhausted. My body was almost limp. Then a wave of energy came about me. I felt good again. I felt calm and at peace. I knew I had done the right thing. I looked up and smiled. A cardinal again came flew close enough for me to almost catch it. For sure it was someone talking to me, but who? I said a quick prayer and again thought of Uncle Buddy and thanked him. Wherever he may be.

I went home and entered like the hurricane I was always known to be. Blake was feeding Chaz and startled by my entrance. She had music playing and singing to Chaz as she fed him.

"Maximo!" she screamed and felt my energy. I was so excited and proud of myself that I grabbed her, kissing her like crazy and tickling her to make her laugh.

"Maximo, what happened? I guess it's good? Stop! You're making me laugh so hard. I don't want to drop Chaz!" She was laughing and drunk off my excitement. She pulled away from me, and I chased her to continue kissing her neck and hugging her. She continued to laugh and pulled the bottle away from Chaz who was not happy to stop eating.

"Maximo, stop and tell me what happened!" she said as she walked briskly around the kitchen island to avoid me. She went back to feeding Chaz who was almost done but wanted every last drop. She propped herself against the counter and looked at me as I was smiling and frisky. "Maximo, talk to me please!"

"Yeah, so I went in there not knowing how I was going to feel about the whole thing. I thought that I wanted to work there and was looking forward to an offer."

"Okay, so you got an offer?"

"Oh yeah. They gave me an offer. It was ridiculous. The money was insane, the incentives, company shares, sick vacation time, ridiculous!" Blake watched me and tended to Chaz who was now being burped, and I followed her up to his crib. I was so loud because of my excitement. She gave me a signal to bring down my volume while she told me in her eyes that she approved of what I was telling her.

"Okay, so you took it?"

"No. I didn't. I take the proposal and ripped it in their faces. I told them they should be ashamed of themselves for never reaching out or supporting me. You know that Dan went and talked to the media about me saying that he thought I was guilty? So, I left and threw the paper in the air and left. I left. I'm done!" She put Chaz down and walked over to me right into my arms.

"So, you're done?" she said in her seductive voice, coming in for a kiss.

"Yes, Blake, it's me all day and all night now. What do you think?" She didn't answer and kissed me. It had been some time since we were able to be intimate together. Today that all changed.

After a long afternoon of being back learning Blake's body all over again, we ended before dinner with a much-needed shower. It reminded me of the one I wanted to take with her in Montana. She didn't disappoint.

There weren't many words; we attended to Chaz who lost our attention for the past few hours. I got him ready for bed and put him down for the evening. Blake was ready for more as she waited for me to come back down. Her hair was wavy from not blowing it out after the shower. She wasn't wearing any makeup. I could see through her shirt. She gave me the dazzling eyes that invited me to come straight to her. I picked her up and pushed her onto the island, and we continued where we left off that afternoon. She was warm and gentle with me. I was freed from the pressures of the firm and released from the burdens of people degrading me. Each time she gave me tension, it was a surge of that power to be freed. No one can make me feel like Blake.

She sat on the island in my arms as I caught my breath. She was pleased with our performance. I was pleased with making up for all that time lost.

"I am proud of you, Maximo. I like that you stood up for yourself. I believe in you, Maximo, whatever you do."

"I thought you would be proud of my new moves. I had a lot of time to think about all the things I want to do to you. So, you like it? Alright, I know now how to change up my game. I want to make you happy." Deflecting again. I know, I need to work on this. She lifted her head back to face the ceiling and groaned at my sarcasm. She also can't resist it at the same time.

"Maximo, you know what I mean. Can you be serious for like a hot second?"

"Ohh the groans, the hot second. Serious? Alright. I got it. You need me to be serious. I wasn't for the past few hours of taking care of you.

Alright, pumpkin, you got serious." I went in deep for a kiss and grabbed her back into me. The round was going to start again. She laughed and tried to push me off, but she was weak. I wore her out.

"You know what I mean, Maximo." She didn't stop me from taking advantage of her. But I did need to answer her. I did need to figure this out.

"Blake, I'm not sure. I know I need to figure something out. My name is out there. People love me. People have been me. People hate me. People are not sure what I'm about but want to know. It's a lot to process. What's next? Will someone hire me? Am I a risk or not? I think I need to work for myself, but I'm not sure just yet what that is. I think some time to let the buzz settle down is what I would like to do and stay here with Chaz. I know you're itching to get back into the office. I see how you keep going into your laptop and making all your checkup calls. Go back and I can stay here. I know you have a big meeting next week. You can focus on that. I really want to enjoy Chaz. What do you think?"

"I think that it's good for you to take time to be with Chaz and for yourself. You deserve it. You have worked hard your whole life. I do want to get back to work. I do miss it and have to start to concentrate on our big meetings coming up. I hope that you won't get bored with this. I'm afraid of you falling into a rut. I worry about you."

"You always take care of me. I won't. You won't let me. I will find something to do; I will. I can even work on some of your projects if you want. Imagine me working for you? Oh, I'm such a bad employee. I'll have to be scolded."

"Maximo!" She ended the conversation, and we went upstairs.

CHAPTER FOURTY-ONE

~

Kelsey was born on a hot day in July, unexpected and ready to conquer the world. She made us smile from the moment she was born. Our family was perfect. I was juggling both kids, and Chaz was now running around and getting his hands into everything. Kelsey wanted so much attention, and she was so cute I couldn't resist her. It was hard for Blake to get herself back to work after Kelsey was born. I was already in a routine that just received an addition that loved to make sure we were on schedule with her plans, not ours. I didn't mind. It was the family life I wanted.

Each morning Blake went to give Kelsey a feeding before heading into the city. She kissed them both goodbye and lingered around some mornings when she had trouble leaving. I reassured her it would all be okay. Then she caught up her courage and went on her way. I hated to see her struggle like that. It hurt me to watch her in pain. I sent her pictures and videos all day long to make her feel that she had not missed anything. She will not miss a beat. Some days I pack her a lunch with love notes in it to keep her interested in me. We have date nights to keep us being us. Our routine was solid for the next few years, but it grew weak between us.

Weekends Blake encouraged me to go and play golf with some friends. It gave her time alone with the kids.

"Where are you going to play today?"

"Jax's country club. He got us a later tee time, so I'm in no rush this morning. What do you all plan on doing today?"

"I'm going to take the kids to the park. Chaz can play on the swings while Ms. Kelsey can play in the sand. I caught up with the ladies, and some of their friends will be there. It will be nice to catch up with them. So, I'll see you for dinner tonight?"

"Yes, I want to have some alone time with you, Blake. Our schedule is daunting for us. It's not giving me enough Blake time. I miss you."

"I look forward to it. I miss you too." She came in for a kiss. I was starting to get afraid that we were drifting apart. I thought of my parents and wondered if two kids were too much for them. Did the problems start when Nico came into the picture? What were their problems? I didn't want to go down that path. We were both tired at night. Date nights were now quick dinners and a glass of wine and then a race home to pay the babysitter. We were so tired by then we went straight to sleep. I knew that I was looking at other women. Blake was so beautiful and worked hard to get back in shape, but it was just more time away from us. I was also not in the physique I once was. I eat junk food on the go. I don't get to the gym as much as I used to. I wondered if she doesn't think I'm as attractive as I once was? Does her mind wander and look at other guys? She was in a land of men all day. I was in a land of babies and married women. The temptation was always out there. I regrouped and looked at Blake. I brought her in for a kiss and another one.

"Let's go upstairs for a few minutes. The kids can watch TV. Look, they're content. Come on, I miss you." She hesitated and rested her head on my chest. I nudged her again. I needed to feel her so I could get thoughts of other women I was tempted by in my daily life out of my head. She looked at the kids. Chaz was content with Cheerios and Duck Tales. I walked her up the stairs and held her from behind as I slipped off her skirt and then her top. She held her hand to reach to play with my hair from behind. She was lost in the moment. I was self-conscious about where she was. It was silent and gentle. I was afraid to make it dangerous today. I was suddenly afraid of where we were as Maximo and Blake.

When it was over, she put her clothes back on quickly and didn't look at me. My feelings were hurt. She was holding back. I grabbed her hand as she was about to leave the room. I sat on the bed, and I know fear was in my face. I needed reassurance.

"Blake, was that okay? You're so quiet today." She smiled and looked at me. The reassuring kiss was there.

"Maximo. It is always a treat to be with you. I'm just tired. I have a bad feeling about today. I don't know why. I'm sure everything is fine. We're just going to the park. I haven't been out with the kids in a while. But, I mean, maybe you could use some new tricks, kid. You're getting old and need to keep up with me." She leaned into me and forced my body to lay back onto the bed. She pushed herself on the right spots to make sure I could feel her. We kissed again and I turned her around on the bed. I stopped and looked at her, pushed her hair away from her face, and felt her energy. She blinked long blinks with a smile.

"My game is weak, huh? Well, then I will have to work on that. Maybe tonight I'll show you some new tricks. Can you maybe stay awake for that?" We laughed.

"Oh, Maximo. I am ready to see you step it up. I'm a tough judge, you know. Are you sure tonight? Short notice, you're going to be out all day. Maybe you will need a nap this afternoon?"

"Look at you, alright, pumpkin. Game on. Don't cry when you ask me to stop because you're exhausted." I stepped up and walked downstairs as we both laughed at each other. I was foolish to think someone else could ever replace Blake. The thoughts are gone from my head. I grabbed my clubs and headed out the door.

When I arrived at the golf club, I noticed that my phone died. It had 100% battery when I left the house. I had no idea what happened. I went to plug it in, and it still didn't work. Nothing I could do about it now since we were next in line to tee off. Jax let me use his phone to text Blake that my phone was dead, and I would go to the store when I was done. She didn't reply.

Our foursome teed off and my game was on point. I was making the par 4s and even some par 3s. It must have been the reassurance from Blake this morning. I daydreamed about her as the other guys complained about their wives. I couldn't wait to get back to her and the kids. We drank beers and after we finished the 18th hole, we went to the clubhouse for some scotch. Jax's wife and her girlfriends came over to join us for a round. The day was perfect. Just enough of a breeze for us to enjoy the course without breaking a big sweat. I was in the moment. The ladies were thirsty. For drinks, yes, but they were also divorced. They were thirsty for some new blood. They had no problem flirting with me. I brushed them off. I had this morning with Blake to remind me that tonight was going to be better than that, and I was so in love with her and she was just distracted. I would have pounced. I was that weak. I didn't see how strong our love was.

One woman was taking the ice out of my drink and sucking on it when I looked over. She reminded me of Ramona. It was her sad desperation for my attention. I had to laugh when I looked at Jax. He nodded his head, thinking the same thing. It was my cue that it was time to leave.

"Jax, did Blake ever text you back?" I asked him to let them know I was a happily married man.

"No, sorry Bro."

"Alright, I'm going to head out and get my phone fixed and get dinner started. You know, do the Dad thing."

We slapped hands and said our goodbyes. I went into the bathroom and suddenly had a knot in my stomach. Maybe it was the bad wings I just ate. I got to the bathroom and threw up. I felt light-headed, and if I didn't know better, it was like I had just gotten beat up. My head hurt and my stomach. I threw up again. I was drained. Great, now I am getting sick and will have to cancel tonight.

Blake, don't be mad at me. I'm with kids all day; I'm bound to catch a bug.

All I heard was silence. Maybe she expected me to disappoint her.

I went to the phone store that had a long line of problems to be solved. People were taking forever to decide between the I7 or I8. Ugh, I was agitated and not feeling well. The woman Alice from the table came into the store. I think she followed me.

"Maximo, are you going to buy a new phone?" She got in close to me. It was uncomfortable.

"Yeah, this one is busted. I want to get a new phone and get out of here. We got big plans tonight with the family so I want to rush there." I tried not to look at her. She was standing so close. I kept looking up, searching for the line to move so I could just get myself out of there. The bug I had was starting to surface again. I did not want to have to leave to race home to the bathroom without a new phone. She could see the sweat beading up on my forehead.

"Maximo, you don't look so good. Are you okay?"

"Yeah, I'll be fine." My place in line was next. I pushed her out of my way and went straight to the counter. The phone was busted; I got a new one and held it together to calm my body down. The nauseous emotion went away. Alice lingered around the store browsing phones. Did she honestly need one? My phone was set up, and I had a slew of messages. A few were unknown numbers. One was from Blake, then a bunch from Jax. Something was wrong. I listened to the latest one first.

"Mr. Cruz, this is the police. Your wife and children were in an accident. Everyone has been admitted into the hospital. Please contact us right away." I didn't need to listen to the rest. I ran out to head straight to the hospital. I brushed past Alice. She screamed out to me and chased me into the parking lot.

"Maximo, where are you going so fast? What happened?" She was not going to stop following me. I stopped as I opened my car door.

"My wife and kids were in an accident. I don't know what's wrong. I'm heading to the hospital." I slammed the door and fumbled to turn the car on and get into gear. I raced myself there with nothing else on my mind but my family. I couldn't live without my family. I needed for them to be okay.

I entered the emergency room, searching for my family, and asked the nurse at the desk. "Mr. Cruz. Your wife and son are over there." She escorted me to them. Blake had a horrible gash on her head and was bandaged up. She had cuts and scrapes and was sleeping. The doctors were concerned she had a bad concussion. The sleeping made them nervous, and she was closely monitored. Chaz was next to her, all cut up with a broken arm. He was awake but out of it.

"Chaz, where is your sister?" The nurse answered that she had to have emergency surgery and was in there now. She had ruptured her kidneys, and they had needed to take her in right away. All I could do was sit and wait. I held Blake's hand as she slept. I prayed for her to awaken. She was so soundly out of it. My feeling in my gut was her. It was them getting into a car accident. Why didn't I listen to the signs?

"Blake, my Blake I love you. Come to me, baby. I'm here for you now, baby. I'm praying for Kelsey. She's going to be okay, I just know it. I know it, Blake. Listen for my voice and come to me, baby. We need you. Kelsey needs you." After a few chants, Blake opened her eyes. I was there for her.

"Kelsey! Chaz!" she mouthed but her brain wanted her to scream.

"Blake, you are okay, my love. You are okay. Chaz is right here. I moved my head so she could see him. He was asleep at this point.

"Kelsey," she said as she looked at me.

"Kelsey is in surgery. We need to pray for our baby. We need to pray that she will be better." She closed her eyes again and went to touch the bandage on her head to acknowledge the pain she was feeling. I took her hand away and held them both.

"Are you in a lot of pain?"

"Yes." It hurt so much to see my family hurt. But they were alive. That was all that mattered right then.

"Yes, Maximo. Where were you? I called for you," she asked in her strained voice and eyes closed. She held onto my hands.

"When pumpkin? When? I sent you a message. My phone had died when I got to the course. I sent you a message through Jax's phone. Didn't you get it?"

"No." She moved her head to face the other direction. I have disappointed her.

"Blake. I swear my phone died. I left you a message through Jax. I thought you would have seen it. I had a horrible bug this afternoon. I think it might be from feeling that you were in an accident. Oh, baby. I'm so, so, so sorry. We have to be strong for our kids. I'm here for you all. This is where I want to be. I was insecure this morning. I didn't take heart when you said you were worried about today. Your intuition is amazing. I'm so sorry for not feeding more into it."

"Maximo, you were so distant with me this morning. I felt as if you weren't interested in me anymore. I felt you with someone else. Are you with someone else? Please tell me the truth." She always knows what I'm thinking; I didn't realize she could feel right through my thoughts.

"No, my love. It's always you. Always. We have so many challenges since Kelsey. She is beautiful and funny. She reminds me of you every day. I think we fell into a rut. I have not and swear I have not cheated on you. When we are not together, my mind drifts but always comes back to you. I promise you. I don't want someone else. I promise." She turned her head to face me again. She opened her eyes and squeezed my hand.

"Blake, I wonder all the time if I'm good enough for you. When you go into the city and meet fabulous men, do you think I measure up? I've gained weight. I'm with kids all day. Can I carry a conversation that suits you? Do you miss the times before me? Before our family? I always am afraid of not being good enough. I love our life. But I miss us being intimate. I miss us. I would never want anything to happen to our kids. It breaks my heart to see you all like this. Blake. It's always you. I promise you, it's always you." We held hands and she kept her eyes open enough to look at me and see that I was genuine. Then she turned her head to someone behind my shoulder. It was Alice from the country club. From the Verizon store. It was her.

"Alice? Why are you here?" Blake knew who she was.

"Why Blake. I was with Maximo all afternoon, and he ran to be here. I didn't know what happened, so I followed. I want to be supportive. I just had to come and see if you were okay. How are you doing honey?" I was shocked. Blake looked at her then at me. I turned white.

"I am…You were with Maximo?" She spoke over me as I couldn't get the words out.

"Oh, we all met up after their golf game for some drinks. Then to get his phone fixed. I want to make sure you are okay, hon." Blake looked at me upset. I was white and embarrassed. She was lying, but Blake believed her. This is beyond borderline crazy.

"Maximo? You were with her all afternoon?" I looked down and shook my head with my hands over my eyes. I was pissed.

"Blake, I played golf with Jax and a few other guys. She was there with his wife. They sat with us for a drink. I just met her. Then I ran into her at the phone store. That is it. She followed me here. Blake, you know I would never lie to you." I was acting guilty. I didn't hear Blake's call when she needed me. When the kids needed me. I felt guilty. Blake was upset.

"Oh, I'm sorry. I was just worried about Blake, so I came. Blake, honey, I hope that you feel better. Sorry to disrupt you. Let me know if you need anything. I'm going to go." She rubbed Blake and went on her way. Blake was so upset she started to cry. I went to hug her, and she pushed me away.

"STOP, STOP," she said and pushed me away. "I needed you today, Maximo. Where were you? With her? I worry about someone stealing your heart all day. Now here it is. Maximo, please just go. Leave us alone. Just leave us alone. I don't want to see you." I didn't know what to say. Blake cried and wouldn't let me touch her. I looked back at Chaz who was now back awake and watching us. I felt like I just lost everything.

"Blake, I love you. You're upset. Nothing happened, love. Nothing. I will go and wait for Kelsey. We'll get through this. That woman is a crazy, desperate single woman playing a mind game on you. I don't know why she came."

Blake cried and looked the other way. "Isn't there always a misunderstanding with you, Maximo?" she said to me. She was right.

I looked back at Chaz who was listening to the whole conversation and not understanding what was happening.

"Please, Blake. Believe me. I love you. I do. I have to go and wait for Kelsey." I kissed Chaz and asked him to take care of his mom. He nodded. I went to kiss Blake even though she wouldn't look at me. I had to fix this. I went into the waiting room for Kelsey. I turned to God and I prayed. "Lord, please take care of my family. How does this happen to someone twice? Please take care of my Blake. I don't want the trauma of a second accident to hurt her further. We need her for Kelsey. We need Kelsey to be okay. Lord help her be okay. Let everything with Chaz be okay too. Help us break through this. I never cheated on Blake ever. I will never. Help her to believe me. Lord, help me get my family back." I repeated this over and over again. I need to believe in us again.

After about an hour of me pacing and freaking out, the doctors came out to look for me.

"Mr. Cruz? Mr. Maximo Cruz?"

"Yes, that's me. How is Kelsey? Is she going to be okay?"

"Hi, Mr. Cruz. Yes, she is okay. We took out the obstruction and were able to patch up the kidneys. It will be some time before we see if they will respond. She's young, so hopefully her body will go into a strong development mode and recuperate from this. It is not guaranteed."

"Ok, thank you. So, what is the worst-case scenario?"

"The worst-case is that she has to go through dialysis and possibly a bag. She may have to have a strict diet for the rest of her life. Let's not get ahead to the worst. Let's focus on the best. She came through. She's alive. Focus on her being happy and healthy. Keep the positive energy."

"Thank you, Doctor, I will. Thank you so much. Can I go and see her?"

"She will be out of recovery soon. Go pop your head in and say hello. She's coming out of anesthesia and will need a familiar face. She'll be in a room soon."

"Thank you. I will." I ran into the recovery room where the nurse escorted me. Kelsey was sleepy and not sure what had just happened. She was scared.

"Kelsey, baby girl. Daddy's here." I held her hand as she was startled. She was not sure what has happened. It was overwhelming. She saw me and started to cry. She called for Blake.

"Momma, momma! No, no. Ahhhhhh!" she screamed. I did my best to calm her down.

"Kelsey, Kelsey. Listen to my voice. You're going to be okay. You are okay. Daddy is here, my love. Calm down and listen to me." I rubbed her arm since I couldn't pick her up and bring her into my arms. It killed me. She slowly calmed down as I worked with her on the breathing methods that Blake had taught me. She listened and eventually calmed herself down. She held my hand and went to sleep peacefully. I stayed with her for a few hours and fell asleep until a nurse woke me up.

"Mr. Cruz, she's going to be fine. Your wife is having night terrors and screaming for you. I think you should go there." I stood up abruptly and gave Kelsey a kiss. She was in good hands. I needed to be with Blake now. The nurse escorted me down the hallway as we did a brisk walk/run to Blake. Chaz was awake and helpless, but he was attentive and watching her. He was too young and too restrained to know what to do. When I entered the room, Blake was screaming out of control and crying. She was still in a sleeping state. She screamed out for me and for the kids. Was she reliving both accidents? I came to her and held her close. I talked her through it.

"Blake, my love. Listen to me. Listen to my voice, stay with me. Blake, I love you. We all love you. Everyone is going to be okay. Kelsey is going to be okay. Chaz is here with me, and he'll be okay. Blake, come back to me. I'm here for you. I love you. I need you; our kids need you and love you. Blake, you are safe. Follow my voice, love, come home to us."

She tormented herself for a bit more and then calmed down. She never woke up again that night. The fear of the concussion and possible coma was starting to feel real to me. I needed to send my positive energy to her. I needed to stay in faith and pray. I fell asleep sunk into her hospital bed, holding onto her with Chaz in the bed behind me.

In the morning she twitched and finally awoke. It startled me also to wake up.

"Maximo."

"Yes, love. I'm here. I'm not leaving you. You're not getting off that easy. Blake, I love you. I love our family. I'm never leaving. Never."

Chaz awoke and looked up and wanted to get in close to listen. He was still so small but so brave right now for his age. I felt his energy and turned to him and smiled with the reassurance that it would all be okay. He smiled. He was happy and fell back asleep.

Blake was weak. The nurse came by to check on her. She had calmed down by then and was falling back asleep. The nurse needed me to walk away for her to check on Blake. I took the moment to run to see Kelsey. She was in and out of sleep.

"Daddy, Daddy," she cried when she opened her eyes.

"Sleep, my love. Sleep. Chaz and Mommy are okay. You're going to be okay. Tell your body to heal and heal fast so you can come home and be happy. We can do the park and have ice cream. What flavor is your favorite again? I forget."

"Daddy, you know I like strawberry. How can you forget?"

"Oh, look at you, Ms. Kelsey. I didn't know if maybe you changed your mind since you've been here. You have grown up so much. I wasn't sure. Strawberry it is."

"Daddy, what happened? Where are Mommy and Chaz? I'm scared." She was so young and innocent.

"Lovey, you were in an accident. Mommy and Chaz are okay. They can't see you because they're also hurt, but they're okay. You'll see them soon. Be strong, my love. Get better so we can play in the yard, eat Cheerios, and watch cartoons in the morning. Ask God for everyone to be okay."

"Yes, Daddy. I will." She went on to fidget with her blanket and doll. She closed her eyes and held her promise. I felt her pray. I felt it was safe to walk away then and get back to Blake.

Blake was awake and feeling much better after rest. The fear of a coma and concussion miraculously were wiped away. It was another miracle. Breakfast came, and Chaz and Blake ate together. I was not invited. Chaz was still smiling; even in his pain, he was happy. Blake didn't look over when I was there. It hurt. I gave them both kisses and went back to Kelsey who slept soundly. I slept next to her on the futon.

Blake and Chaz were released a few hours later and came to meet up with us just as Kelsey awoke. I was beat but would not admit how tired I was. Kelsey was more herself today; she was recovering nicely according to the doctor. Blake insisted on staying with her and that I take Chaz home. I didn't want to upset her. As much as she needed to get home, I listened and gave them both kisses goodbye. Blake was still angry with me.

I got a babysitter for Chaz and returned in the afternoon. Both Blake and Kelsey slept soundly. I sat and watched until they awoke. Blake opened her eyes and smiled when she saw me. I reached out for her hand. We went for a walk to get something to eat as Blake needed nutrition to gain her strength back.

"Blake, are you going to be mad at me forever? I don't know what to do here." We sat at a table in an awkward cafeteria of people sad and awaiting news. Maybe not good news. I was a piece of that category.

"Maximo, I have something to tell you."

"Okay, what is it?"

"Maximo, I'm so ashamed. I didn't know how to tell you this. A few weeks ago, I had a dinner for work, you remember?"

"Yes, for the export business. I remember. The gentlemen from Denmark came into town?"

"Yes, that one. Well, we've been distant from each other for some time now. I think we've both acknowledged that. I was starting to look at other men, and I hate that I was. I always want you, but I felt that I lost you. I was very flirty with these men as I was looking for attention. It was disgusting. I didn't even know I was doing it. But then all the moms keep telling me how fabulous you are. I come home and you want to go to sleep. You stopped touching me; I missed that. I should have brought you to the dinner, but I didn't because I felt that our energy together is so off everyone can feel it. I thought they would see that, and it would ruin the deal. I flirted, not thinking of it as anything but flirting. But it was the wrong signal. After we signed the deal, we had drinks that turned into one too many. One gentleman was into me. I liked the attention, but all I wanted to do was to come home and be with you. I was weak; I was drunk. He grabbed me for a kiss, and I was caught off guard. I ran away; I ran home to you. I'm so ashamed. The next day I ripped up the contract and told them I could not do business with them. I'm so ashamed, Maximo, I am.

"I love you, Maximo, I do, but we haven't been intimate for months. I was afraid you were pushing me away. You're enjoying this life with the kids and having fun. I love my job and I love to work, but I wasn't having the fun. I felt like I had become a boring, unattractive woman. All the moms tell me all the time how great you are and how much fun you are to be around. I don't get that. I get the 'I am so beat' then you head up to bed. I'm scared. When we had this accident, someone else was talking to me, and it wasn't you. Why wasn't it you? When did I become so unattractive to you? Are you interested in someone else? Is it Alice? Please, please just tell me." She looked down ashamed.

I sat back in astonishment. We lacked communication. Our fears were in the same place. As out of sync we thought we were, we were really in sync.

"I don't know what more to say. I'm not interested in those women. Most of them are divorced and just hungry. I like the attention, don't get me wrong. But when you look into it, they're all lacking something. Alice is the perfect example. They see me as the fun guy and have an attraction to that. It's not what I want. They are lacking and think I will fill their void. I don't want to.

"I didn't think we were in a bad place; I think we have a great life and a fun relationship. But you're right. We fell into a rut. I think we need to change our lifestyle. I think I should find a job and maybe we can get a nanny. Is that the answer? I love you, Blake, I don't blame you for what happened. But I'm upset that your lips touched someone else. I'll need time to get over it."

We sat in silence looking somewhere else for the rest of the meal. We both lost our confidence. We both lost our sense of working as a team. I had to get it back. I was so mad.

"What happened with Alice? Why was she here?" Blake asked, scared to know.

"Blake, I told you. I was playing golf with Jax and a few other guys. We had an awesome game. We really did. Then his wife came over with these women, and they sat down with us for a drink. Alice was so heavy flirting, but I didn't want it so I left. I got sick in the bathroom. I thought I caught a bug. My phone was dead. I tried to plug it in, and it didn't work. She followed me to the store. It was so sad. Of course, the store is crazy crowded and when I got my new phone I had all these messages. I ran to the hospital, and she must have followed me. Chicks are crazy. So I think it was insane for her to come here. But they have some balls these divorcees. I'm not interested in her, Blake. No one can compare to you." She nodded her head reassured, but she was still uneasy.

"Thank you, Maximo. It was hard to see that, but I believe you. My mind wanders. Let's not lose each other."

"I agree."

CHAPTER FOURTY-TWO

~

After a few weeks, Kelsey came home from the hospital with a clean bill of health. She was going to be fine. It was a miracle! Blake took time to recover, and we did our best to get back into being us. We went on real dates and spent time with each other. We made love a few times a week and made us a priority. Blake did more of the mom chores, and I held back. I needed to find something to do to occupy my time. I went on job interviews. Everyone wanted me as I had become famous of sorts. I just wanted a low profile. I needed to regroup.

One evening the doorbell rang after the kids went to bed. I went to answer it as Blake was upstairs. It was my mom.

"Hello, Maximo." She looked weak and was holding herself up against the door frame. I didn't know she was coming.

"Mom, what are you doing here? Are you okay?"

She was struggling. "Maximo, are you going to invite your mother in?"

"Yes please." I had to help her walk to get her over to the couch. There was something seriously wrong. Blake came down the stairs and was also astonished at our visitor.

"Maria! Hello! What a nice surprise!" As she came closer, she opened her eyes wide and acknowledged that something was wrong. Mom needed help to walk and help to sit down. I noticed that she had become frail, and I could feel the bones in her back. Blake ran to get her some water and came back to sit on the chair beside us.

Mom needed a moment to sip her water and gather strength enough to talk. It was not going to be good.

"I needed to see you and spend some time with my grandkids. Is that okay?" She wanted to avoid the topic. The anger in her voice showed that she was hiding what was going on. Blake and I looked at each other, not sure what to say.

"Momma, of course. Yes, stay as long as you like. The kids will be so excited to see you. But Mom, you don't look well. Are you okay?"

"No, Maximo. I'm not okay. I'm dying. I don't want to make a big deal about it. I settled my affairs in Miami, and I want to die in peace with my family." I tensed up and held her to me. Blake moved in to console her as well. We all were upset.

Blake went to set up the extra bedroom that she stays in while she's here. I'm about to lose my mom. I don't know what that feels like. We got her into bed and said our good nights. I hoped that this would not be good-bye. Not today. We went upstairs and tried to talk in a whisper. We were afraid of what was happening.

"Maximo, what do you think she has? She looks awful. Do you think she'll go to the doctor?"

"I have no idea. I've seen her in bad shape, but this is a sickness, not a depression. I don't know. But I have to take care of her. Blake, this is my mom. I don't know what I'll do if she dies. I'm not ready for this."

I started to hyperventilate, and Blake came to me to calm me down. I didn't sleep that night. I went down to my mom and sat at the side of her bed. She was sound asleep. Her snores were deep; her breathing was heavy. It was troublesome to watch. She awoke when she felt my presence. She smiled and held my hand.

"Maximo, be strong. Be strong. Thank you for taking me in."

I held my emotions in check. "Momma, what happened? What do you have? I need to get you to the doctor. I want to take care of you."

"No, Maximo, I've made up my mind. It's time for me to go. I have lung cancer. They said it will be quick, and it's too late for treatment. Too many years of smoking. Tell your father to quit smoking, please. No one should die like this."

"Mom, I can't lose you."

"Don't worry, Maximo; I'll make sure to haunt you." We laughed as I am sure she would.

"No, Maximo, I'll always be in your heart. I'll always watch over you and Blake and my fabulous grandkids. It'll be my honor. You were always in my heart, Maximo, always."

"I'll take care of you, Momma. I will." I gave her a kiss and went into an empty corner of the house to cry. I couldn't handle this. When I went back into bed, Blake opened her arms to me, I snuggled in. I needed her right now.

We got Mom a walker and a hospice nurse to come and help with caring for her. I called my dad to come and visit with her as she requested. They always loved each other. Even when they were with other people, they still loved each other. I will never understand how they hurt each other and still loved each other so deeply. It was not for me to understand. I liked how they were now. There was peace. Nico came to visit. He didn't handle this so well.

Blake kept in touch with all of my family and made sure we saw each other on holidays. She held us together. That Easter, we had one last meal with my mom. Kelsey sat on her lap and sang to her all the songs from her favorite Trolls movie. Mom smiled and listened. She had an oxygen tank to help her breathe during the day. She took it off at night, hoping that the disease would take her away. I sat with her each evening until she fell asleep. I combed her hair with my fingers. I prayed that she could get better and stay with us longer. She didn't. It was a cold evening. It was my birthday. She went off in the night. I felt her body give out as I fell asleep holding her hand. Sitting aside her. She was gone.

"I love you, Momma, I always will."

CHAPTER FOURTY-THREE

~

It was morning. I knew it was time to get up, and the alarm was about to go off any second. I was stalling. I didn't want to go through today. I missed my mom; it was hard to go through this. Today was the day I was going to bury my mother. Blake could tell that my breathing was getting heavy. She was awake, faking it until I got up, so she wouldn't upset me. My anxiety was growing. She went back to caressing me and giving me soft kisses. I held onto her tighter. She was my best medicine.

I got up from her embrace and went out the sliding door onto our deck. The rain was heavy, washing away any trace of snow that we had lingering. I took the same deep breaths that Blake was taking, trying to get me to relax. I am always following her lead. Kelsey came running into the room when she heard us moving about. She came right up to my leg to hug me. It brought tears to my eyes, remembering that I'd never be able to hug my mom again.

I picked up Kelsey since she was still small enough. Her curls were long and crazy first thing in the morning. Her smile was so warm. I needed her right now too. I cherished these morning moments with her. Blake ran into the shower, and I woke up Chaz on my way to get breakfast started. He was already walking around his room like a zombie. He wasn't good with mornings; neither was Blake.

"Come on, Buddy, let's go get breakfast." He heard my voice, and we headed down the stairs. I could not make much conversation this morning. What am I going to say for my mom's eulogy? My relationship with her was like a roller coaster. But she always knew she was going to have me. She always believed in me. So many times in my life she was my best friend. I stared at my kids as they ate away innocently. Blake came down to take over so I could get ready. I went into the shower and sobbed where no one could hear me.

We got dressed and headed to the car where Blake took the keys away from me and insisted that she drive. I agreed. I was weak today. Blake knows how to take care of me. I looked through the side mirror to admire Kelsey reading a book in her car seat. It was upside down, but she has it memorized. She is talking to herself and laughing. Her hair is thick like mine; her skin is golden like mine. Blake is pale; Chaz is pale. He is tall like me but is so much like Blake. He has her warm heart; Kelsey has my charm. It scares me. She knows how to steal the show just like I used to. I hope that I can get that sense of myself back. One day it will come back. Blake is so patient with me; I have no idea how she deals with me.

My dad met us at the church with his latest wife of about five years. I believe she is a keeper. The Maria and Dario show had been over for so many years that I was used to our broken family. I will do my best to keep mine together. Blake was my rock; I would strive to be hers forever. Chaz was old enough to understand what was going on; Kelsey was still not sure. I wonder if she'll remember today. I wonder what's going on in her head. I wonder if she'll be as beautiful as Blake when she gets older. I'm overprotective of Kelsey. I kept my focus on her to take my mind away from the event we were about to take part in.

It was cold and damp out. The chill didn't leave your body. I had trouble breathing through this. Blake helped me as she held tight on my arm and tapped me to follow her breathing. I heard the priest speak at the coffin before it was dropped into the ground. I listened for the silence. I heard birds chirp and I looked around and found my cardinal again. It stopped to look at me; I looked at him. I knew everything was going to be okay.

We dropped our roses onto the casket. Blake held onto me as I was not strong in this moment. I called out again to my mom and slammed my fist into the ground. Chaz and Kelsey stood next to us along with my dad. They gave me the moment I needed. It was so hard to say goodbye, but it was time. Blake helped me to the car, and I sobbed into her neck. I don't know how to let go.

CHAPTER FOURTY-FOUR

~

We held the luncheon at our house after the last flowers were dropped onto the coffin. My family was odd. Jax and his wife and kids were there. My dad and his new wife. Blake kept us together for holidays and special occasions. Is this in the category of a special occasion? Aunt Doris came in; Jose came with his family. They lived not far from us. My mom's friends came from Miami and her boyfriend. I just kept making polite small talk and listened to the stories. I was distracted by the sounds of the children running around the house. It was still too wet outside from all the rain for them to play out there.

I glanced from time to time at the empty bedroom downstairs where my mom stayed right before she passed away. I caught myself looking for her to walk out holding onto the walker and sliding it across the wood floor that now had so many scratches between her room and the bathroom. I didn't care. It left her memory. Some moments I swore I heard her. I sharply looked into the room and when I didn't see her, I scanned the room. Blake always caught my eye. She gave me a smile and made sure she took a deep breath so that I would do the same. She knows how to calm me. I re-entered the conversation, and Blake went back to hers.

The food was served, the party was underway; before you knew it, the guests started to leave the house. The people dwindled. I continued to look around, lost in any conversation I had; Blake again gave me the reassurance I needed, and I went about my way. The tables the caterer brought blocked the direct line from the front door through the kitchen to the living room where Blake was stuck. I said my goodbyes to everyone at the door. The knot in my stomach was pounding with intensity.

I became anxious, not sure if I wanted people to stay or to leave. My kids' voices as they ran around in the living room were so loud. My dad was playing with them. I was overwhelmed. The plates clanked in the kitchen as the caterers cleaned up and started to fold up the tables. All these noises were so loud. I concentrated on Blake, who was in deep conversation with my dad and his wife.

"Blake, Blake" I called to her in my head. After a few moments, she caught my eye and turned to me. I was then intercepted by Aunt Doris, so Blake went back to her conversation.

"Oh, Maximo. How are you doing? You don't look so good." I took a sip of my coffee and jumped from the heat.

"Aunt Doris, I'm okay. Just tired. It's been a long journey."

"I know, it has. You were so wonderful to take your mom in and care for her. I know it wasn't easy at the end. She loved you so much. You were always in her heart even before you were born. She always believed in you. Never forget that."

Her words touched my heart so deeply. The knot in my stomach became harder to hold onto. I started to feel weak. Drowsy. Blurry. Kelsey danced her way over to me as the tables continued to be folded away.

"Daddy! Daddy! Look at me, Daddy!" Kelsey screamed as she jumped in front of me to grab my attention. I looked for Blake. I couldn't find her. My vision was still blurry. When Aunt Doris said her goodbyes and left, I could hardly close the door. I felt like a tower about to fall. I was fading.

"I love you, Maximo." I heard coming from the bedroom downstairs. With my cup in hand, I stumbled over there to find the voice. Kelsey, still jumping for my attention, followed me. I was dripping in sweat; my vision was going. Before I got to the door, I heard the walker coming out of the room, and I fell to the ground. My hot coffee spilled in my face and all over my arms.

"Daddy! Ah!" Kelsey screamed and screamed as she cried. I heard voices scatter. "Mommy! Mommy!" Kelsey screamed. The caterers came running, my dad and stepmom, and of course my Blake. I heard them all. I wanted to get up and hug Blake, sit in her arms and cry as she comforted me. I couldn't move.

"Maximo, Maximo! Can you hear me?" My dad was smacking my cheeks to get me to come to. I heard it. I was moving from the reaction, but I didn't feel it.

"Did he have a heart attack?" a caterer asked. My stepmom grabbed the kids and took them into the other room.

"Maximo, my love, Maximo. I'm over here." And behind my closed eyes, my mom was sitting there in front of me and holding my head.

"Maximo don't be sad. I love you, Maximo. I'm okay. I'm finally happy. I had you; I always knew I would have a beautiful son. I had you. You made me so proud. You gave me my future, my hope for life. I always admired you. I was complete."

"Momma, why? Why?"

"Don't look back. So much anger. So much heartache. Don't waste your time on the bad times. Focus on all the good times we had. Be everything to your family. Look up. Look at that woman sitting next to you. Look at how she looks at you. She loves you. Your kids love you. Make peace with your dad; don't be just an acquaintance. We made mistakes. Learn from them. Keep love in your heart, Maximo. I'll always be with you."

"Momma, Momma!" I screamed and jerked up to look for her, but she was gone.

"He's having a seizure!" another caterer yelled.

"No, no, no! He's fine. Please, help me prop him against this wall. Someone get me ice and some water." They scattered about. Blake sat in front of me and opened my shirt.

"Should I call 911?"

"No! He'll be okay. I know he'll be okay," Blake said as she held my face. When she was handed the bag of ice, she put it on the bump on my head. I blinked through my glasses to make sense of the blur and saw Blake. She smiled, we did our deep breath routine, and the crowd relaxed.

"How you doin' pumpkin?" she asked with a smile. I smiled back and didn't answer. I was pale and out of sorts. It was the release I needed.

"Should we take him upstairs to bed?" my dad asked.

"No. Let's get him to the couch." With the help of my dad and the caterers, Blake had me carried to the couch as if I were the body in the *Weekend at Bernie's*. I sprawled onto the couch with my head resting in the corner pocket. Blake took off my shirt stained with coffee and wiped off the liquid from my arms. The crowd gave us what privacy the downstairs could allow. I was her patient. She took my glasses off and placed them on the side table.

"Are you maybe ready for a scotch and a nap?" she asked with sarcasm. I took a deep breath without her reminding me. I nodded yes. She prepared my drink just as I liked it and handed it to me. I held it on my chest, not feeling strong enough to hold it in the air. When my strength was built back a little, I took a sip and helped relax Blake enough for her to move away. Kelsey came running over and crawled on the other side of the couch until she could make her way to me with her favorite Trolls doll.

"Princess Poppy and I want to take care of you," she said. I smiled and made room for them to snuggle with me and my scotch. Blake looked over from the distant corner, and I gave her a wink that I was okay. She went on to escort out the rest of the guests and attend to the caterers. I was at peace.

CHAPTER FOURTY-FIVE

~

The noise level in the house started to fade as our family left our house from celebrating my mom's life. I was falling asleep on the couch and pushed my scotch to the end table before spilling it all over me. Kelsey was getting antsy laying by my side. I slowly dozed off. Chaz played with his toy car on the couch in front of me. When Blake was done with the caterers and saying goodbye to my dad and his family, she came over to check on us.

"Mommy! Can we watch a movie?" Kelsey asked, and Chaz shook his head.

"Yes, lovies… Come, let's give daddy some rest." She picked Kelsey up gently out of my arms and escorted them into the den. I could faintly hear them, but I was already in a trance that I could not break out of. There was a scatter of feet in and out of the room and whispers to make sure I would not wake. I could still hear them, but I could not react.

"Maximo, get your rest. Don't dwell on me." My mom came to sit next to me.

"How do I keep Blake without forever being a disappointment to her?"

"You're not a disappointment to her, Maximo. It's all in your head. She loves you. You know that. Look at how she cares for you. Don't dwell on this, Maximo. Don't become me. Don't do that to your children.

They're so young. Don't lose them. Let's get you out of this depression. Get up and go to Blake and your kids. Enjoy each moment and let go of the past."

"Momma! Momma..." Then she was gone. I woke up to see Kelsey standing in front of me with her troll in tow.

"Daddy, who are you talking to?" she asked me. Blake and Chaz stood a few steps behind her and also wondered what I was screaming about.

"Just having a dream. Come here, sweetheart." I signaled for her to come in for a hug. I needed a hug from her. I didn't want to go back into my depression. As she came in for a hug, Blake and I caught eyes, and she smiled. I smiled back. I wanted this to end here.

"You know your grandma?"

"Yes. Where is she?" She peeked to glance into the bedroom from our view on the couch, but she could not see it. The last few weeks she hadn't come out of the room at all; she was just too ill.

"Kelsey, she went to go live in heaven." Blake sent Chaz over. I moved for everyone to join me on the couch. We hadn't talked much about death to them yet. They were still so young.

"Do you know that she was my mom?"

"No," Kelsey said.

"Yes, she was my mom. So now she's gone, and I'm just sad. I had a dream that she was here, and I wanted to try to hug her one more time. So, that's why I was screaming." Kelsey came in for a hug.

"Daddy, you can have my mommy if you want."

"Your mommy? Is she for sale? Are you giving her up?" We laughed and wondered what was in her head.

"NO!" Kelsey said loudly as she was catching on that we were making fun of her. "No, Daddy, you can borrow my mommy when you need to. She's on loan; you can't keep her!" It still made us laugh. Her wisdom at this age still shocked us. But she was cute and genuine.

"Well, that is very kind of you to share. Sharing is caring you know." Blake smacked my hand since that is the line she uses on the kids all the time. Well, it's working.

"I will for sure use your mommy when she's available, you know, for daddy stuff." I smirked at Blake. She smirked back.

"Alright, all young kids, time for bed. And my oldest kid—"

"Yes?" I answered waiting to be scolded. She gave me a smile as the kids started to run up the stairs for bed. I grabbed my scotch, sat back, and gave her a nod. She nodded back. My Blake was already helping me out of this depression. I closed my eyes and drifted back to us.

CHAPTER FOURTY-SIX

~

The house had calmed down after everyone left, I had another chance to doze off on the couch. My scotch still sat on the table next to me. I moved myself to the living room to fix the furniture we moved for our guests. I put a fire on as even in the sharp spring air, the rain made it chilly. I was relaxing and letting go. I'm not going to let this take me into another depression. Not this time.

Kelsey and Chaz freshly from a bath looked over the railing and in soft whispers yelled back to Blake, "Mommy, he's still awake on the couch, look! Can we do it now?"

"Yes, now go, go," Blake responded and pushed them to move down the stairs. She watched from above.

Kelsey's wet hair swung into my face. She loves to twirl around, not understanding that her wet hair, even dry hair, flies and smacks you in the face. As painful as it can be, it is endearing. She's too young to understand. Today is not the day to explain. Chaz held a thin boxlike wrapped item and handed it to me. Kelsey handed me a small box also wrapped. "It's for you, Daddy!" She looked up at Blake who's watching from the upstairs railing.

"Go ahead and open it!" Chaz said. I looked up to see Blake smiling over me again. They jumped up and down in between Kelsey's twirls. I sat back, not expecting any of it.

"Come here and open it with me," I said as I grabbed both of them to sit on my lap and help me open the wonderful gifts they presented me with. Slowly the paper was ripped away to find the most precious items—a new sketch pad and set of special pencils and erasers for sketching. My old sketch pad and pencils lived in Miami with my mom and were now in a box somewhere with the rest of her things. I hadn't sketched since I was in college. I had given that side of me up. It was an invitation that only Blake knew I needed when it would be the right time. I looked up and mouthed a "thank you" to her with a kiss. She sent a kiss back and came down the stairs to sit with us on the couch in front of the fire.

"Daddy, can you draw me?" Kelsey said and got up to do a dance for us.

"I can, but you can't move around. I won't be able to trace you!" I said back to her as we all laughed. They were so precious. I couldn't bear not having them in my life. I was not going back to that dark place.

Blake, please don't let me go back there, I said in my head. Blake grabbed my hand. She always knew how to take care of me. I'm the luckiest man in the world.

"Alright, the excitement is over. We all had a very long day. So, say goodnight again and off to bed." Blake shuffled the kids into their beds and came down to join me with a glass of wine as I finished my scotch, and we watched the fire crackle before us.

"Blake, you're amazing, I don't know what I would do without you," I said as I pulled her close and soaked her in.

"I know you don't. So, don't find out."

"Blake, my love. I won't go back there again."

CHAPTER FOURTY-SEVEN

~

After the funeral and after the nasty spill I took, I picked up the sketch pad and started to draw again. I drew Blake in all of her detail and glory—I drew her asleep, in the midst of her cooking, and her naked beside me in bed. She was my favorite distraction. I was consumed with my Blake again. She gave me the space to be lost in my sketches. I was in my own world, and she was okay with it. I took the sketches a bit further and rented a studio to concentrate on my painting. It had a new life. I kept my paintings all to myself, hidden away from my family. I wasn't ready to be vulnerable with them as of yet.

We spent quality weekends together, heading to the shore to play on the beach. We spent Blake's birthday weekend at her favorite spot. Now she shared this place with Kelsey who also enjoyed the sunshine and the sand in her toes. Kelsey sparkled like Blake. Chaz was awkward like me, but he had his own personality. He was a bit of a loner. He was just like me. I sketched them sleeping at night. They were my angels.

When I got up the nerve to feel good about my accomplishments, I took Blake on a picnic to the studio. I had decorated the studio with tea lights to catch the right shadows for my grand review. She was blindfolded and loved what she saw when I took off the mask from her eyes. It was a tribute to her, to our family. She took in each painting with touches to the canvas, stepping back and admiring them all. It was a fairytale to her. I just wanted her to know that I loved her. She felt it. We danced; we made love on the floor. We were back to being Maximo and Blake.

After a few days, Blake and I were in a honeymoon phase. The kids felt it. They danced with us as we made dinner. They enjoyed our late nights as they listened and giggled. We were the family dream that I wanted. Blake surprised me one day with a blindfold and took me and two giggling kids to her secret. They were excited. She took off my blindfold as we stood in an open storefront. The kids waited for my response. I didn't understand what it was. I looked around and soaked in the space.

"Daddy, Daddy! Do you love it?" Kelsey asked. I grabbed to pick her up for a hug. I looked around again with Chaz and Blake smiling at me. "Why, I always wanted an empty room." I asked in sarcasm, not sure what to say. I looked to Blake for direction.

"Maximo, it's a gallery. I bought you a gallery to sell your paintings. It's right near the studio. I hope that you like it. I think you found your calling."

"Wow, I thought they were for fun, but yeah. I'd love to sell them. Blake, this is amazing. Thank you!"

"I always believe in you, Maximo. Never forget that."

CHAPTER FOURTY-EIGHT

~

We had the gallery opening, and all of my friends and family were there—Nico, my dad and his wife, his kids, Mazzy and Zac, and Jax and his wife—everyone we loved. It was the wedding we didn't get a chance to have. The paintings sold, so it was time to create new ones. The kids played together—this was the happiest occasion. I took Blake to the balcony with a glass of champagne to soak in the moment of joy with her.

"Blake, thank you so much for this. Thank you. I love you so much. This is the best thing ever."

"Maximo, I love to see you happy. I do. I have something to tell you."

"Should I be afraid?"

"No. I had a dream last night, and I know who the voice was that came to me the night of my accident with the kids. I never met him, but I need to tell you who it was."

"Alright Blake, who?"

"It was Uncle Buddy. He came to me when you couldn't. He told me when we got into the accident that we would all be okay and that you had me in your heart always. He's our angel." There it was. She said it. It all made sense. Uncle Buddy was our angel. I had glimpses of him and our conversations when I went to pray and a cardinal came to visit me. It was him all along. He was our angel. Thank you, Lord, for blessing me with an angel.

"That's awesome, Blake. Wow, he is our angel. I can't believe that." Blake danced in my arms, and I admired the sounds of love and laughter from inside. "I have everything I need when I have you, Blake."

That night I went to bed with Blake in my arms and had a dream. It was Uncle Buddy standing next to the car talking to Blake, consoling her. She was knocked unconscious. He placed his hand over her, and she was able to wake up. He looked at me and winked as he disappeared. He was always an angel. I saw my mom wave in the field as I chased Blake and the kids; we were one. I laid in the field with Blake next to me. "You're always in my heart," she said, and I closed my eyes to drift off into a deep sleep.